Also by Barbara Williams
The Crazy Gang Next Door

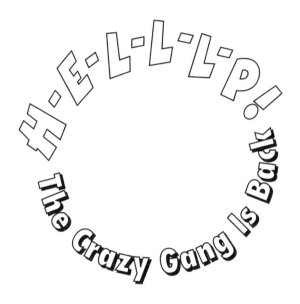

H·E·L·L·P!
The Crazy Gang Is Back

BARBARA WILLIAMS

HarperCollins*Publishers*

Library of Congress Cataloging-in-Publication Data
Williams, Barbara.
    H-E-L-L-L-P! the crazy gang is back! / Barbara Williams.
        p.   cm.
    Sequel to: The crazy gang next door.
    Summary: Kim finds out to her horror that two members of the
Spikes gang have transferred to her junior high school and that one
of them has a crush on her.
    ISBN 0-06-025887-X. — ISBN 0-06-025888-8 (lib. bdg.).
    [1. Schools—Fiction.   2. Humorous Stories.]   I. Title.
PZ7.W65587He   1995   95-18980
[Fic]—dc20   CIP
                                                                              AC

Typography by Darcy Soper
1   2   3   4   5   6   7   8   9   10
❖
First Edition

For Cindy, Gil, and Jeff
who prove how much fun a crazy gang can be

1

■ ■ ■ ■ ■ ■ ■ ■ ■ ■ ■ ■ ■

Splut! Kjuk! Scrut!

Mr. Silcox was in the middle of calling the roll for first-period geometry and hadn't even reached my name—Sanders, Kimberly—when the intercom sputtered and a deep male voice boomed over the loudspeaker.

"Good morning, scholars. This is your vice principal, Mr. Tempest, speaking. The principal, Mrs. Marler, has left the school grounds on an unexpected errand, so I want to welcome all of you to Bryant Junior High on her behalf. I hope you'll all enjoy the year here at Bryant. Now for the bad news. The Welcome Day assembly, which was scheduled for this afternoon, has been canceled. Repeat: Today's assembly has been canceled, so the class periods will be the regular length. That's all. Have a nice day!"

And the intercom clicked off.

"What?" cried a girl.

"They can't call off the assembly," complained someone else.

Groans went up all over the room.

I don't suppose anyone cared too much about the cancellation of the Welcome Day assembly, which was never exactly class-A entertainment—just six student body officers standing up to introduce one another and brag about how smart and hardworking they all were. What everyone did care about was attending classes for the regular length of time. We never had to do that on the first day, since every class period was cut by half to make time for the Welcome Day assembly at the end of school.

I may have been the most disappointed person in the room. I'd been waiting all summer to talk to my third-period English teacher, Mrs. Paddock. And if classes were going to be the regular length, I'd have to wait nearly an hour longer than I'd planned in order to see her.

"Cripes!" I complained to no one in particular. "This school always holds a Welcome Day assembly. Every year."

"Not when the new student body president is drunk," said the kid behind me.

I turned around and rolled my eyes to let him know what I thought of his stupid joke. I'd gone to school with our brand-new president, Ernie Crenshaw, since kindergarten and knew for a fact that he'd worn a plastic ink protector in his shirt pocket ever since the second grade. "Earnest Ernest" we called him behind his back. "Funny," I sneered. "Very funny."

The kid raised his right hand, like a Supreme Court justice of the United States being sworn in. "Trust me," he said. "I saw him staggering into the boys' room. Totally sloshed."

"I don't believe you," I said. And I didn't. The queen of England was more likely to stagger into church for her grandson's baptism. Our dweeby new student body president wouldn't take a sip of anything stronger than 2% milk the first morning of his reign.

"They were all higher than kites," said the girl across the aisle. "All of the student body officers. Someone broke into the room before their break-fast meeting this morning and put vodka in their orange juice. Mrs. Marler had to drive every one of them home."

I tried to think of all the kids I knew who had been on school detention last year and were capable of various felonies, but not a single one of them hated the student body officers or Mrs. Marler or even Bryant enough to play a trick like that. Not on the first day of school. People always loved the first day of school because classes were short and teachers never gave homework and everyone could show off their new clothes.

"I heard that when Mrs. Marler arrived for the meeting, Ernie Crenshaw was throwing doughnuts at the clothes hook on the wall and the rest of the officers were balancing plastic cups on their heads while they snake-danced barefoot around the room," said another guy. "Can't you just picture the look on her face?"

The thought of Mrs. Marler bursting in on that scene was enough to make anyone laugh, so we all did. Even Mr. Silcox smiled, though you could tell he was trying not to.

"*Quiet!*" he commanded. And after everyone settled down, he finished calling the roll. Then he handed out our books and told us what pages he wanted us to read. But I couldn't concentrate on geometry or on drunk student body officers, either. I couldn't concentrate on anything but Mrs. Paddock, my third-period English teacher who also happened to be the adviser for the student newspaper. On my lap I crossed the fingers on both hands. *Please!* I thought to myself. *Please, please, please.*

CRASH!

Something came hurtling through the window, sending splintered glass in all directions, like spray from a blue whale's blowhole.

"*Eee-ow!*" screamed a girl a few seats away from me. "Someone hit me with a brick!"

"I'm bleeding!" yelled a boy.

"Me, too!" shouted people from all around the room.

"Someone get the janitor to come clean this place up," hollered Mr. Silcox, which a couple of boys seemed happy to do. As they left the room and ran down the hall, Mr. Silcox dived into his desk drawer, pulled out a box of Band-Aids, and began dealing them out like cards from a deck.

Until then, no one had noticed the girl in the corner of the room. Her hands covered her face, and she was sobbing hysterically. "No! No! No!"

Mr. Silcox rushed over to her. "Are you all right?" he asked.

"No! No! No!"

He took her by the shoulders. "Were you hit, too?"

"No! No! No!"

Desperately Mr. Silcox looked upward, as if asking the ceiling for advice. Then, for no reason, he pointed at me. "You!" he ordered. "You take both of these girls to the nurse's room and get them taken care of. The rest of you turn to page 4 in your books."

A big egg was forming on the forehead of the girl who'd been hit by the brick, and her cheek was dripping blood. But she was clearly in better control of her senses than the girl who was crying. Together we eased the hysterical one out of her seat and half pushed, half dragged her toward the nurse's room.

While the nurse rushed to prepare an ice pack for the bruised forehead and an antiseptic swab for the bloody cheek, I tried to get the other girl calmed down.

"Are you hurt?" I said.

"No! No! No!"

"Why are you crying?"

"She found out where I am!"

"Who found out?"

"She did. She hates me. She's hated me ever since I told on her for setting the girls' room on fire." The poor girl was raving. I could barely understand her.

"Who set the girls' room on fire?" I asked patiently.

"She did. When she went there to smoke her pipe. I changed schools just to get away from her. But she found me, anyway. She threw the brick."

I wanted to tell her to stop being paranoid, that

nobody likes paranoid people because they always seem so interested in themselves. But I figured that might not be a polite thing to say to a total stranger, especially one who was already upset. So I just rephrased my earlier question. "Who hates you?"

"She does. DeVeda."

My stomach flipflopped. DeVeda? I'd met a girl by that name myself and I'd had my own run-ins with her.

Actually, to be exact, I'd had my run-ins with DeVeda and her three goony brothers—Earl, Calvin, and Bubba Joe. That bunch of redheaded delinquents had found the keys to Mrs. Overfield's duplex next door while Mama and I were taking care of it, which gave them the opportunity to commit a million crimes. They'd taken Mrs. Overfield's 1965 Thunderbird on high-speed joyrides around the city. They'd stunk up her state-of-the-art walking shoes by wearing them on their smelly feet. They'd used her priceless antiques for ashtrays and then tried to hock them at a cheap secondhand store in Park City.

But it didn't seem likely that my DeVeda was the same one as this girl's. It was true that DeVeda wasn't an ordinary, vanilla type of name. Still, there had to be dozens of DeVedas in an area the size of Salt Lake.

"DeVeda who?" I asked.

"DeVeda Spikes."

I gulped. That was my DeVeda, all right. There couldn't be two girls named DeVeda *Spikes* in Salt Lake. But even though I knew she could invent new sins to commit faster than fleas could hatch on a dog's back—even though I knew it was exactly like her to throw a brick through the window of her own school—it didn't make sense that she'd travel all the way across town to do it to someone else's junior high.

"When was the last time you saw her?" I asked.

"Last May. She put a dead mouse in my back-pack. She stuck my gym shoes to the floor with Krazy Glue. She—"

"Listen," I said, trying to cool her down. "I think maybe DeVeda reformed last summer. I happened to see her in the ZCMI snack bar at the end of August and she was a totally different person." I didn't bother to mention that the reason DeVeda might have seemed different was that she had been in the company of a well-dressed lady who was probably her mother.

The girl looked doubtful, and she opened her mouth as if to argue with me. But just then the nurse walked over to bandage the rest of her assembly line. "Well, did the brick hit you, too?" she asked me.

I held up an arm to show her my Band-Aid. "No, I just have a little scratch from flying glass. My teacher told me to bring the other girls to see you."

"Well, you better get back to class. Second period started fifteen minutes ago. Didn't you hear the bell?"

"Cripes," I said. "Señorita will have a fit." I waved good-bye to everyone and started off on the run for second-period Spanish.

WHOO-OOP! WHOO-OOP! WHOO-OOP!

I hadn't even reached the B corridor when the alarm sounded. Doors banged open, and kids spilled out of rooms like water through the holes of a sieve. I guess they figured they deserved a little time off from classes today, the Welcome Day assembly being canceled and all. Everyone was laughing and joking and elbowing and I got carried along in the flow until we reached the sunshine outside.

"What's going on?" someone asked. "They never have fire drills on the first day of school."

"Maybe it's a real fire," someone else suggested.

"No way. Schools never have real fires."

"This one is real," a boy shouted excitedly. "I was there when it started. A redheaded girl in science class lit a match and blew up the lab."

I felt someone smacking my arm with a book.

"Redheaded girl!" screamed the girl I'd taken to the nurse's room. "I told you DeVeda had followed me! She's trying to get even because I reported her when she set fire to my last school! I made my mother talk to the superintendents of two different school districts so I could transfer to the farthest junior high school in the whole county. But DeVeda Spikes followed me! She'll always follow me! I'll never be safe anywhere in this entire state as long as I live!"

With that, she threw all her books and papers and pencils on the ground and charged off toward the Utah Transit Authority bus stop on South Temple, whizzing through the school yard like an Olympic medalist.

It was the last time I ever saw her.

2

You could tell it wasn't going to be much of a fire. There was only one fire engine and hardly enough smoke to blacken a catfish. Pretty soon people got tired of watching and started milling around to look for their best friends.

Since I'd given it to her for her birthday two weeks earlier, I recognized Darci Decker's denim shirt with the Native American bead trim. "Darci! Darci!" I waved. "Over here."

Darci pushed her way through about a million bodies to find me. "Oh, Kim. Isn't this dumb? A little science lab explosion interrupting things the very first day of school! You should see the guy who was sitting next to me. Oh, he's so *kee-yute!*"

Darci and I feel the same way about lots of

things—from clothes and movies and rock groups to teachers and Hawaiian pizza. Nearly everything, in fact, except boys. She has absolutely zero judgment when it comes to the male species. I rolled my eyes, imitating her pronunciation. "You think all boys are kee-yute."

"This one is really great. You should see him. Only trouble was, he wouldn't even look at me. He was too busy slobbering in the other direction. At Ashlee Brinkerhoff."

"Ashlee Brinkerhoff? Is she in your second period?" I was glad that I didn't have to sit next to her again. Ashlee had sat behind me last year in Utah history, but she had considered herself much too cool to talk to me. The only time she realized I wasn't invisible was when she wanted to borrow my notes or get help for an assignment. Once she even got me into trouble by copying my answers, word for word, on a test. "Any boy who slobbers over Ashlee Brinkerhoff is definitely not cute."

"I can't believe you'd say that." Darci cocked her head at me. "You and Ashlee certainly have the same taste."

"What's that crack supposed to mean?"

Before Darci could answer, our friends, Brynne and Jannalee, hurried over.

"Did you hear why the Welcome Day assembly

was canceled?" Jannalee gasped. "Earnest Ernest was drunk!"

"Isn't that a hoot?" said Brynne.

The four of us, plus Mimi Saltzgiver, had been friends since elementary school, so we all knew Ernie Crenshaw personally and shared the same opinion of him. Which means that none of us had voted for him in the student body elections last May.

"No way," I said.

"Give me a break," said Darci.

"Drunk as a skunk," Brynne insisted. "I know what you're thinking, but everyone's talking about what happened this morning before school. Someone slipped into the student body officers' room before their breakfast meeting and spiked the orange juice. When Mrs. Marler showed up, Ernie had peeled down to his undershorts and all the officers were dancing the lambada on the table."

I couldn't help wondering if Earnest Ernest wore Superman undershorts, even though I knew this latest rumor was more preposterous than the one I'd heard in first period.

"Just because everyone's spreading rumors doesn't mean they're true," I said out loud.

Jannalee poked Brynne. "Tell them what you saw."

Brynne took a deep breath. "Well," she began. "I came to school early to put up some posters in my new locker, which is right across the hall from the student body officers' room. I'd just finished and was ready to go meet Jannalee when this kid came tiptoeing out of the room with the sneakiest look on his face you ever saw." Brynne bobbed her head smartly and then looked around the circle at the rest of us, as if she'd just explained her brand-new scientific theory for the origin of the universe and were waiting for applause.

"Is that all?" I said disgustedly.

"Who was he? What did he look like?" asked Darci, who is always interested in persons of the opposite sex, whether they're among the FBI's Ten Most Wanted or not.

"Well," said Brynne, squinching up her face to think, "he had biceps like watermelons. And freckles the size of pennies. And curly red hair."

"Oh," I moaned, and grabbed for my stomach, where a prickly cactus was suddenly growing inside. Brynne was describing Earl Spikes! If DeVeda Spikes had really followed the girl in my geometry class to Bryant this morning (of course she hadn't, but if she *had*), it would be just like her to bring her personal bodyguard along—namely, her brother Earl. That redheaded ape had nearly broken my arm last summer when he twisted it behind my back.

"You look as if you just saw a ghost," said Jannalee.

"Do you know him?" asked Brynne.

"No," I said, hoping like anything that I didn't.

"She does, too!" said Darci. "She's got a megacrush on him. We saw him in ZCMI last summer, and her face turned the color of ketchup. She wouldn't even introduce me to him. It took me three weeks to find out what his name is. Earl Spikes."

"I don't have a crush on Earl Spikes!" I raged.

"You do, too," said Darci. "You said he was kee-yute."

"*I did not!*" Of course I hadn't said that. I'd lie on a bed of nails with elephants dancing on my stomach before I'd say a thing like that. Earl Spikes was a Neanderthal with half the IQ of a sesame seed.

"Yes, you did," Darci argued. "You said that on a scale of one to ten he was a seven."

Well, yes. I might have said *that,* but of course I hadn't meant it. Darci had been the one who said Earl was cute, and not wanting to insult her taste or anything, I'd sort of agreed with her. Besides, I didn't mind having her think that I knew a boy she didn't.

"Well, Earl Spikes couldn't have spiked the officers' orange juice this morning," I said. "He doesn't even go to Bryant."

"Too bad for you." Darci sniffed.

Brynne and Jannalee had grown bored with this conversation about a guy they'd never met. "Oh, look!" said Jannalee. "There are some kids from the Bowling Club. Let's go tell them about Earnest Ernest."

And they left us faster than they'd arrived.

I was so mad at Darci I could have kicked her, but if I went on talking about Earl Spikes, she'd just be more convinced than ever that I liked him. I decided to change the subject. "How come you said I have the same taste as Ashlee Brinkerhoff?"

"Because you're wearing the same sweater today."

"Oh, you're kidding! Tell me you're kidding! She'll think I bought it just to copy her!" I looked down at my brand-new sweater from Nordstrom, which had cost three times as much as any other sweater I'd owned in my entire life. It was an off-white hand-knit wool with a fantastic Hopi design in turquoise and red. Mama had said that it wasn't practical (and even I could tell it was too hot for the first day of school), but I'd promised to take good care of it and even pay for the cleaning bills if she'd buy it for me.

Darci shrugged. She didn't care if I'd copied Ashlee or not. "Those firemen sure are taking their time." She looked at her watch. "We've missed all of second period and half of third."

"Not third period!" I cried. "We can't miss third period!"

"How come?"

"I have English from Mrs. Paddock third period. I've been waiting all summer to find out if she's chosen me for editor of the *Bulletin.* I can't stand it if I have to wait another whole day to find out."

Darci groaned. "Not that again. I can't believe you dropped out of cheerleading tryouts last spring just to be editor of the school paper."

"I've already told you. I want to be a writer when I grow up. Like my mother."

"There's no law that says you can't be the *Bryant Bulletin* editor and a cheerleader, too. We had so much fun this summer at practice. And it will be even more fun now that school has started. You could have made the squad easily."

"Maybe," I said.

"We're having practice today after school. Did I tell you that? None of us can walk home with you."

Twice, I thought. She'd already told me twice this morning while we were walking to school. But I decided not to remind her. "Are you sure my sweater is exactly like Ashlee Brinkerhoff's?" I asked.

"Positive. Uh-oh. Speak of the devil . . ."

Ashlee was walking straight toward us, a big grin on her face. She patted my back. "Oh, Kim! What a darling sweater!" She put her arm around me and stroked my shoulder.

She'd never been this friendly to me before. What was she up to? "Yours is nice, too," I said lamely.

"Thanks." Ashlee tossed her head so the whole world could enjoy her gorgeous black hair. "I guess we both have good taste." She winked at me.

I tried to smile. "I guess."

"Have you seen Mrs. Paddock yet?" Ashlee asked.

My heart thumped. "Uh . . . no."

"She told me she wants to see you."

I was really smiling now. "She did?"

"She has good news for you," Ashlee said.

I've won! I thought. Ashlee is being friendly to me because she knows I'm going to be the editor. She's hoping I'll forget all the mean things she's done to me and give her a job on the paper.

"Well, see you around. 'Bye now." Ashlee skipped off with a dainty little wave.

"Oh, Kim!" said Darci. "What's on your sweater?"

"Huh?"

"You've got something on your sleeve."

I looked down. There were brown smudges on the sleeve and shoulder of my wonderful new sweater.

"Ashlee!" I raged. "Where did she go? I'll kill her!"

Darci squinted as she looked around. "I don't see her. Uh-oh. There's a huge spot on the back, too."

I bent my arm, held the sleeve to my nose, and sniffed. "Chocolate! Ashlee got chocolate all over my sweater. On purpose." I'm dead meat, I thought. Mama will have a cow when she finds out.

"The stains might come out," Darci said. "There's a new cleaning company on Thirteenth East that my mother says works miracles. Of course it's a little expensive."

I thought about the lunch money in my purse. Maybe if I went without lunch for a couple of days I'd have enough money to get the sweater cleaned. Maybe this new cleaning company really could perform miracles. Maybe I wouldn't even have to tell Mama what had happened.

The day certainly hadn't started out very well, but things were bound to improve after I'd been to see Mrs. Paddock. I could hardly wait.

3

Mrs. Paddock was bent over her desk, writing with one hand and eating a sandwich with the other. Watching her made my stomach rumble.

"Oh, Kim!" she said, looking up. "Come in."

"I'm sorry to interrupt your lunch period, but—"

She nodded toward the empty chair by her desk. "Sit down. Care for some potato chips?" She held the package toward me.

I took one eagerly. Then she pushed her sandwich aside. "This is my preparation time. My lunch period isn't for half an hour, but I'm completely off schedule today. That fire during second and third periods threw everything out of whack."

"Yes," I agreed. "I was sorry to miss your English class. But Ashlee Brinkerhoff said you wanted to see me."

"Yes, yes. I'm glad you got my message."

The second hand on the quartz clock on the wall bumped around the dial, and I shifted nervously in my chair.

But Mrs. Paddock seemed at ease. She folded her hands on her desk and stared at me over the rims of the narrow reading glasses perched on the end of her nose. She smiled. Under her halo of white hair her blue eyes twinkled. "Well, I guess you'd like to know why I sent for you."

"Uh . . . yes."

She reached for a file folder on her desk and riffled through it. "I wanted to congratulate you on this wonderful essay you submitted for the *Bulletin* editor competition. All the teachers who read it were very impressed. You did a solid job of research, and you expressed yourself very skillfully."

I've done it! I thought. I'm the new editor!

I wanted to jump up and down and sing and fly out the window and soar among the seagulls that were circling the school grounds during lunch hour.

"Thank you," I said.

"So we've chosen you for the associate editor." She held out her hand. "Congratulations."

Associate editor. That wasn't what I'd hoped for,

but I could live with it, I supposed. In a way it might even be better than editor. More writing, maybe, because there would be less editing. Less supervising.

"I know you'll do a wonderful job," she added.

"Thanks," I said. "Who's the editor going to be?"

"Ashlee Brinkerhoff."

My stomach rumbled again, but not from hunger. "Ashlee? But she didn't apply."

"Of course she did." Mrs. Paddock looked down.

"Not before the deadline," I argued. "I talked to you the day after the application deadline. You told me the names of all the people who had applied. Ashlee's wasn't one of them."

She fumbled with her file folder, straightening the pages inside. "Oh, surely I mentioned her."

"No, you didn't. I would have remembered. We had a long talk about it. Fifteen people applied, and you read me all their names."

"I must have been careless. I'm sorry."

I bit my lip, wondering what you were supposed to do when you knew your teacher wasn't telling the truth. At least not the whole truth. I'd listened specifically for Ashlee's name when Mrs. Paddock had read me the list, and it hadn't been there. Period.

The week after the *Bulletin* deadline I'd gone to

the cheerleading tryouts to clap for my friends, so I knew for a fact what a scene Ashlee had made when she wasn't chosen for the cheerleading squad. Had she gone crying to Mrs. Paddock to let her submit a late essay for the *Bulletin* competition? Had she made her mother call the principal?

Mrs. Paddock took my hand in both of hers. "I'm sorry if you're disappointed, Kim. You and Ashlee both submitted wonderful essays, and the committee was sure either one of you would make a fine editor. We wrestled with our decision for three days. But in the end we decided Ashlee's essay was a little more factual—a little more mature."

I pulled my hand free. "But—"

"Anyway, I want to congratulate you again," Mrs. Paddock continued. "I know you and Ashlee will have a marvelous time working together. She told me what great friends you are."

Great friends?

I looked down at my expensive new sweater and the chocolate stains Ashlee Brinkerhoff had deliberately put there.

I had coaxed Mama to buy the sweater because I was sure this would be the happiest day of my life, and I wanted to be wearing something special to remember it by. This was the day I had looked forward to all summer. This was the day Mrs. Paddock

23

would tell me I had been chosen as the new *Bryant Bulletin* editor.

If I hadn't been such a coward, I would have looked Mrs. Paddock straight in the eye and told her right that minute that Ashlee Brinkerhoff was a cheating, lying, two-faced rattlesnake and that I'd rather eat live cockroaches than spend a single second as her associate editor. But I was sure I'd burst into tears if I said another word.

So I stood up and hurried from the room, positive that if I lived to be a hundred and ten I could never have another day this bad the rest of my entire life.

4

I sneaked up the back stairs to my room so I could get out of my new sweater before Mama saw the chocolate stains.

"Kim? Is that you?" she called from her office.

"Yeah."

"Come and tell me about school."

"In a minute. I'm just changing."

I stuffed the sweater under the bedcovers, grabbed the first T-shirt I could find, and put it on.

Mama beamed at me when I got to her office. "Well, tell me all about it. How was the first day of eighth grade?"

Before I could answer, there was a terrible noise outside.

Vrmm. Vrmm. Vrmm. Scre-e-e-ch! GRRRRRNK!

"Good heavens!" Mama cried.

We stared at each other in horror.

Then, through the open window, we heard the horn of a 1965 Thunderbird plus Mrs. Overfield bellowing to Mama at the top of her scratchy seventy-six-year-old voice.

Honk! Honk!

"Janice! Janice Sanders!"

You didn't have to be a rocket scientist to figure out that Mrs. Overfield, who lived in the other half of our duplex and shared our garage, had backed her car out of it and crashed into some innocent BMW or motorcycle or wagon parked in our back alley. Maybe even a little kid sitting in a wagon.

"Janice!" she croaked again.

Honk! Honk! Honk!

I took off like a cannonball, my mind racing as fast as my feet. It was only Monday afternoon, for crying out loud. Why was Mrs. Overfield driving her car on Monday afternoon? The only good thing about sharing a garage and alley with the world's worst driver was that you knew she wasn't likely to kill you at any time other than Saturday mornings. That was when she revved up her old T-bird to drive to the grocery store. So if you kept yourself barricaded indoors every Saturday from 9:00 A.M. until 12:00 noon, you were fairly sure of keeping your nerves and bones intact.

With Mama huffing and thumping behind me, I sprinted out the door of her office, down the stairs, out the back door, and across the lawn to the alley, which ran the length of the block between Federal Way and Butler Street.

Mrs. Overfield's head of blue-white hair was hanging out of her car window, but her hands were firmly planted on the Thunderbird's horn.

Honnnnnk!

She removed them at last when she saw Mama. "Oh, there you are. I don't have time to clean up this mess," she explained breathlessly with a quick nod toward the clutter.

The sight wasn't pretty—a couple of overturned garbage cans plus lettuce leaves and corncobs and empty pizza cartons and old rags and millions of gray things that looked like itsy-bitsy pillow feathers scattered all over the place. At least there wasn't any blood that I could see.

"You'll find an old broom on my side of the garage. And a rusty snow shovel to use as a dust catcher." She nodded once again, this time in my direction. "Kimberly will help you."

I opened my mouth to reply to that but couldn't think of anything to say before she screeched her tires and caromed down the alley. Then she suddenly slammed on her brakes, backed up a few feet, and barked another order. "I didn't have time for the kitty litter. Be sure to change the kitty litter."

With another screech of tires she zoomed off again, spraying gravel and carbon monoxide in our faces.

"Bye-bye! Have a good time!" Mama called with a wave. But I stared after the disappearing yellow car with my mouth hanging open.

"Where does she think she's going?" I complained, which was only a slightly more polite way of saying "Who does she think she is?"

"Las Vegas," Mama replied.

"Las Vegas!" I was horrified. In my mind I could see a 1965 yellow Thunderbird knocking over garbage cans and uprooting shade trees and smashing cute little desert tortoises the whole 450 miles from Federal Way in Salt Lake City, Utah, to the Circus Circus Hotel on the Las Vegas, Nevada, strip. "She's driving all the way to Nevada?"

Mama set the garbage cans upright. "No. Just to the Greyhound Bus depot. She's picking up three of the ladies from her Spanish class at the university and driving them to the bus depot. They're catching a Fun Bus to go to Las Vegas for a week."

I guess I should have been relieved to hear that, but I wasn't exactly. There were still hundreds of

people living between our house and the bus station who might want to ride their bicycles at the
side of a road or push their baby strollers across a
street. "You shouldn't let her drive," I scolded.
"One of her other friends could have taken a car.
Or you could have offered to chauffeur them. Why
did you let her drive?"

Mama picked up a smelly old corncob with the
tips of her thumb and index finger and dumped it
into one of the cans. "Actually, it was my idea."

I couldn't believe my ears. My mother had
always seemed fairly smart to me, even for a lady
who didn't know the difference between MTV and
VHS and was born even before skateboards were
invented. But now, without warning, she had gone
completely senile. "Your idea!" I cried. "How
come?"

Mama looked around for someplace to wipe her
corncobby fingers, then suddenly rubbed them
against one leg of her elastic-waist jeans. "Go get
the broom and the shovel and I'll try to explain."

I hurried to the garage and collected Mrs.
Overfield's tools. "Well?" I challenged when I got
back. "How come you wanted her to drive to the
bus depot?"

Mama wiped her forehead with the inside of her
elbow. "Can you lower your voice, Kim? My head

feels like a volcano ready to erupt. It's been a real doozy of a day."

Hmmph. What did grown-ups know about doozy days? I'd practically invented them. Here it was, my first day of school—the day I'd looked forward to all summer—and I get home feeling like the victim in an old Freddy Krueger movie. I took a big swing at a pile of feathers with the broom. A few of them landed in the snow shovel, but most scattered in the air like lazy dandelion seedlings in a gust of wind. "Well?" I repeated. "How come you wanted Mrs. Overfield to drive?"

Mama sighed. "I guess I didn't want to be responsible."

"For driving them to the bus depot?"

"Goodness, no." She picked up a red-stained pizza carton, twitched her nose at it, and dropped it into a garbage can. "For the Thunderbird. I didn't want to be responsible for that car parked a whole week inside our garage while she was out of town. You remember what happened to it the last time she went away."

I shuddered. Of course I remembered what had happened. The gang of Spikes bandits had found the keys, and DeVeda had decided she should be the one to drive—even though she kept grinding the gears and screeching the brakes and driving about a thousand miles a minute the wrong way down the street. At least Mrs. Overfield liked to walk places and never endangered the Earth's living plants and animals except on Saturday mornings.

"You don't really think those Spikes kids might move in next door again!" I said. If I closed my eyes I could still see their faces—Earl's and DeVeda's and Calvin's and Bubba Joe's. They had the reddest hair and meanest eyes of anyone in the whole world. And in just one little month they had invented more crimes than John Gotti and his pals in the syndicate had ever heard of.

"No-o-o," Mama said. "I don't really think so. But you never can tell. I didn't expect them to do it the last time, either."

I nodded. Until you actually met those four Spikes goons, you would never dream that a family of little kids could do the terrible things they did.

"So," Mama continued, "this week while Mrs. Overfield is out of town I'm not taking any more chances. I spent all day trying to persuade her, and she finally agreed to let me hire a locksmith to change all the locks on her doors. He just finished up, not fifteen minutes before you got home."

I nodded again, remembering how I'd seen a minivan—with the words GLEN'S LOCKS printed on the side—driving in the opposite direction as I started up South Temple from school.

"After he left, I remembered the car," Mama went on. "I hadn't thought to tell him about the ignition to the car. But then it occurred to me that if she parked it in one of those big overnight lots by the Greyhound Bus depot, the children would never think to look for it among all those other cars. So-o-o, we don't have anything to worry about." Mama gave me a smug grin.

You had to admire her for all that planning. Not many people would have thought of changing Mrs. Overfield's locks. I probably would have suggested something as lamebrain as rigging all the duplex doors and windows with bullhorns or electric cattle prods or buckets of used kitty litter.

Still, I wasn't so sure about Mama's idea for hiding a car in an open-air parking lot, right out in front of heaven and everybody. I'd heard about car thieves who go through parking lots looking for cars with keys still in the ignition, and our next-door neighbor was just dimwitted enough to leave hers there. DeVeda might even have made an extra set of keys last summer. If she and Earl could find their way to Bryant Junior High this morning, they could certainly find their way to the Greyhound Bus depot parking lot.

I shook my head at myself. Cripes! Of course they wouldn't think to go there! Not in a bazillion years. I was getting as paranoid as the girl in my geometry class this morning. Maybe DeVedaphobia was catching.

I swung my broom at another bunch of feathers. They fluttered into the air like stray ashes from a bonfire as the shovel filled up with heavy gravel. This job wasn't any fun. Why didn't Mrs. Overfield clean up her own messes?

"This sure has been a gruesome day," I complained. "Worse than gruesome. I had to walk home alone because all my friends had cheerleading practice after school. They're going to have cheerleading practice after school every single day, and I'm going to have to walk home alone for the rest of my entire life."

"Well, until football and basketball seasons are over, maybe. But you knew that last spring when you decided to drop out of tryouts." Mama took a package of Doublemint from her pocket and studied it for a minute. "So what else is troubling you?"

What else was troubling me? Exactly everything that had happened the whole day.

"Ashlee Brinkerhoff!" I spat out the name as if it were a cuss word, which of course it was.

"Ashlee Brinkerhoff," Mama repeated. "Isn't she that pretty little thing with the black hair and blue eyes?"

"Ashlee Brinkerhoff is the thing who *boys* say is pretty. Which makes her stuck-up and obnoxious and not the least bit how anyone with half a brain would want to look."

Mama unwrapped a stick of gum and popped it into her mouth. "So what exactly about Ashlee is troubling you right this minute?"

Taking a deep breath, I let it all tumble out at once. Except for the part about the sweater, of course. "I'll hate being associate editor under Ashlee," I finished. "She's the biggest lint-head in the entire school."

"Goodness, Kim, being chosen associate editor of the school newspaper is a wonderful honor. You'll have lots of fun."

"Fun! Working under Ashlee Brinkerhoff?" I thought about my beautiful new sweater and about Ashlee submitting her essay late and about the rotten way she'd treated me all last year. "Besides being stuck-up and bossy," I continued, "she cheats, too. She copied the answers off my Utah history test last spring. Word for word."

Mama shook her head. "I'm glad you weren't the one who cheated. You know how your father and I feel about that. Still, I'd try to forget whatever happened in the past if I were you. People can change. If your English teacher respects Ashlee enough to appoint her the *Bulletin* editor, she must be smarter than you think."

"She isn't smart, just sneaky. And I'm going to be miserable every single minute I have to work with her. I wish she'd just disappear."

Mama picked up a dirty rag and put it in the garbage can. "You should always be careful what you wish for, honey. Sometimes wishes come true."

"*Mom, you're not listening to me!*"

She stopped midbend en route to a scrungy lettuce leaf, stood up straight, and looked me in the eye. "I'm sorry, honey." Pinching her lips into a little knot, she waited for me to go on.

"Oh, I don't know what to *do*! I was really looking forward to working on the paper. But I'd rather die than spend the next nine months having Ashlee treat me like her personal slave."

Suddenly Mama put an index finger to her lips. "Shh. What's that noise?"

I stood still to listen. "The doorbell!" I exclaimed. Someone was ringing our front doorbell more frantically than an ambulance driver sounding a siren on the way to a four-vehicle pile-up. Who could it be at 4:30 on Monday afternoon?

And what was the emergency all about?

"I'll get it!" I dropped the broom and the shovel to the ground and took off as fast as my legs would go.

5

Brinnng!

Bam! Bam! Bam!

Brrrrrrinnnnnnnnng!

Whoever was at the door meant business. And intended to conduct it right away.

I raced across the lawn, through the back door, and along the main hallway. Panting, I opened our front door.

My friend Mimi Saltzgiver was standing on the porch, dressed in a fluorescent pink leotard and gasping like a secondhand truck.

"Where have you been?" she complained. "Like I don't have anything to do but ring your bell."

"In the back alley helping Mama. Mrs. Overfield knocked over—"

"This day has been un*real!* Like the most

impossible day I ever dreamed of." She elbowed her way past me, collapsing in Dad's favorite living-room chair. "The most impossible day of my life, and, like, you don't even answer the door. Promise you'll help me."

"Help you what?"

"I can't talk until I get a drink of water. I ran all the way here, and I've been ringing your bell and shouting for, like, a hundred years. My mouth is so dry I could spit chalk dust."

I started toward the kitchen. "Would you like a Coke?"

"Just water. I'm, like, ready to die from dry-mouth rot."

I got a glass from the cupboard and opened the refrigerator for the water pitcher.

The back door opened. I guess Mama had grown impatient waiting for a report on the noise we'd heard. She looked anxious. "Who was it?"

"At the door? Just Mimi."

"What did she want?"

"I haven't found out yet. I've been too busy giving her first aid." I held up the glass of water so Mama could see for herself.

"Goodness. Is she hurt?"

"Just thirsty."

Mama seemed to lose interest. "Oh. Well, I guess

this isn't the time to continue our conversation about the school newspaper."

"I'll come find you in your office as soon as she leaves."

Mama gave me a quick hug and started down the hall toward the stairs.

I went through the other door into the living room and handed Mimi her water. "Here."

"Thanks." Mimi accepted the glass, guzzled the whole twelve ounces at once, and came up for air with a windy sigh.

"So, help you what?" I repeated.

"I'll tell you on the way. I don't have time to explain now. We've got to go." She set the glass on the coffee table.

"Where? I've got to let my mom know—"

"To Darci's, of course."

I called upstairs to tell Mama where I was going, and Mimi gave me a hefty shove toward the door. *"Come on! I'm in a hurry!"*

Outside, we headed across our front path and up Sigsbee Avenue toward Darci Decker's house on Third Avenue. Mimi was in a hurry, all right, and I had a hard time keeping up with her long legs, which didn't look any shorter in that skimpy pink leotard. I figured she had come straight to my house from cheerleading practice without bothering to change her clothes, which I knew for a fact wasn't her usual M.O. Mimi Saltzgiver had more designer outfits than most movie stars, and changing in and out of them was her favorite sport.

"Will you please tell me what this is all about?" I asked.

"We've got to find out if Darci will, like, really be out for the season."

"Out for what season?"

"Cheerleading, of course. She didn't come to cheerleading practice after school because she had an accident in fourth-period gym and had to be taken to the hospital in an ambulance."

"You're kidding! Is she all right? What happened?"

Mimi stuck out her lower jaw and blew some stray hairs off her forehead. "Her new seps, like, really goofed, I guess."

I'd taken enough gymnastics myself to know that a *seps*—short for biceps—was what people called a jock who gym teachers rounded up to act as a spotter when girls were learning new tumbling exercises.

"What did he do?" I asked.

"I heard at least three different stories. But Jannalee, who's in Darci's gym class, said that he kept getting into fights with the other sepses. He

40

was having a shoving match with one of them when he was supposed to be watching Darci, and he let her fall."

"He sure couldn't know much about spotting. What's his name?"

Mimi shrugged. "He's new at Bryant. Jannalee said he's redheaded and sort of hunky, but—"

I grabbed her arm and stopped walking. "*Oh, Mimi! You don't think it was Earl Spikes, do you?*"

Aside from the members of my family, Mimi was the only person I knew who was actually acquainted with that fluff-headed tribe of house-breakers. My other friends had been away on vacation last July, so she was the only one who had been in the neighborhood when the Spikes imbeciles moved themselves into the other half of our duplex.

"Are you kidding? Earl Spikes is not a hunk. Besides, he doesn't even go to Bryant." She wriggled her arm free and started walking again. I trotted to catch up.

Just as we reached the fork where Sigsbee Avenue runs into Perry and Wolcott, a shiny red convertible with four teenage boys—the driver plus three guys in the back—roared north on Wolcott. The car slowed to a stop when it reached us, and the guys in back whistled and waved their arms and hooted at Mimi. "Look at the pink flamingo."

It was a lousy thing to say, although you had to admit that in that fluorescent leotard, with her two legs as long and skinny as a pair of flagpoles, Mimi's resemblance to the bird was pretty striking.

"Check out those gorgeous gams," one of the boys yelled.

Mimi stuck out her tongue, which wasn't very mature of her. Or very bright, either. Two of the guys in the back responded by sticking their tongues out, too. The third one made an ever ruder gesture with his hand that I'd rather not describe. Then with a squeal of rubber the car sped off and turned the corner to Second Avenue.

Mimi clenched her jaw and both fists. I was afraid she might hyperventilate right there on the sidewalk in front of the house owned by two old ladies who were always running out with umbrellas to chase away stray cats.

It seemed like a really good time to change the subject, so I did. "You still haven't told me what I'm supposed to help you with," I reminded her.

She charged off again, elbows pumping like oars in a canoe race. "Ashlee Brinkerhoff is a—a *mouth*!"

I couldn't disagree with that, even if I wasn't sure how it fit into the conversation.

"That's what *she* called me today. A flamingo."

"When?"

"At cheerleading practice. She had the nerve to show up at cheerleading practice. She told me I looked like a flamingo in this leotard. Then she charged over to Miss Hudson and told her that I had the worst figure in the whole school—no shape at all except for, like, a round belly and knobby knees—and everyone would be staring at me. I'd, like, spoil the effect of the whole choreography."

"Well, you got off lucky. Do you know what she did to me today? She—"

"I'd like to grab that tongue of hers and, like, stuff it down her throat. Promise you'll help me."

"Stuff her tongue down her throat?"

Mimi made a face at me as if she thought my brains were made out of Styrofoam. "Nooo. Try out for the cheerleading squad so I won't have to have Ashlee for a partner. If Darci drops out, Miss Hudson will have to hold tryouts for my new partner. I know it will be between you and Ashlee because you're the only two girls not on the team who can do, like, the splits or a decent backflip. I'll just perish if I have to have Ashlee for my partner."

"Don't worry. She's the new *Bryant Bulletin* editor. She won't have time for cheerleading."

Mimi's eyebrows shot up to her forehead.

"Ashlee's the new editor? She beat you? Why did you let her beat you?"

I counted to three. "I didn't exactly let her."

"Well, all the more reason for you to beat her for the cheerleading squad. Please, Kim. Ashlee Brinkerhoff is the last person in the school I'd want for my partner."

I didn't exactly want her for my editor, either, and I was sure Mimi's chances of working with her weren't as likely as mine. "You won't be stuck. You already have two alternates for the cheerleading squad, remember. Either of the Joslin twins could take Darci's place."

Mimi turned toward me, her face the color of her leotard. "That's what I've been trying to tell you. The Joslin twins are history. Like, totally out of here. You should have heard their mother screaming at Miss Hudson an hour ago."

I tried to picture their mother—any mother—screaming at the head gym teacher. It would be sort of like a poodle yapping at King Kong. "How come?"

"Because Miss Hudson wouldn't let both girls be on the squad," Mimi explained. "Miss Hudson said she'd spent, like, the entire summer working out choreography for a squad of ten girls and she wasn't going to do it all over again just because

Mrs. Joslin wanted both her daughters on the team. So Mrs. Joslin said she was taking the twins out of public school and transferring them to, like, Rowland Hall."

I suddenly bumped into Mimi. "Ooh! I'm sorry." She'd stopped walking. "What's the matter?" I asked.

"Shh." She lifted a finger to point.

Parked right in front of Darci Decker's house was that bright-red convertible full of smart-mouth boys.

"What are *they* doing there?" Mimi crouched down, trying to make those long legs and that psychedelic outfit invisible. "I don't want them to see me. We can't go into Darci's house *now*!"

I looked around for cover. With more energy than I knew I had, I pushed Mimi behind a lilac bush. "You can hide here. Maybe those boys won't park there long. Maybe they're waiting for someone who's just stopping in to check on Darci."

Bingo! As if I'd been looking into a crystal ball, the door to Darci's house opened and Ashlee Brinkerhoff stepped outside. She waved to someone inside the house, then turned and bounced down the front steps, as lively as a brand-new tennis ball.

"Oh, it's Ashlee!" I whispered.

The driver leaned across the front seat of the convertible to open the door and Ashlee climbed aboard. *Vrmmm!*

Mimi, who had already peered from behind the bush to see things for herself, burst into sobs.

6

Darci was crying, too.

Mimi and I had felt more or less optimistic when Mrs. Decker had answered the door and said that Darci was home from the hospital emergency room and in her bedroom. But now that we could see her for ourselves, we weren't so hopeful. She was lying flat on her bed, her left leg propped up on six million pillows with twin ice bags on her ankle and calf.

Mimi, her cheeks quivery and tearstained, looked down at Darci. Darci, her eyes red and puffy, looked up at Mimi. Right on cue they both started crying in earnest. A regular duet.

I studied Darci's pillows and the ice bags while I waited for the sobs to ease up enough to make myself heard. "Are you all right?"

"No. I hate life. I can't believe all the awful things that happened to me today. First I break my leg, and then I lose my place on the cheerleading squad, and now I find out that Ashlee Brinkerhoff—*Ashlee Brinkerhoff!*—thinks she's going to replace me." Darci reached for a tissue.

"I mean, does your leg hurt?" I said.

"Of course it hurts. It's broken in two places. I'd rather have both legs broken than be replaced by Ashlee Brinkerhoff. How would you feel if Ashlee Brinkerhoff got the job you wanted?"

"Well—" I began.

"Can't the doctor, like, put a brace on your leg or something?" Mimi suggested. "Sometimes when we go to those gymnastics meets at the U, the girls are wearing leg braces, and they, like, go right on swinging on the uneven bars."

Darci nodded. "I know. I tried to talk him into that. But he said I needed a cast, and he was going to give me one in a few days, just as soon as the swelling goes down." Self-pity rose in her and turned her voice into a wail. "I'll have to wear it for at least two months."

"How did you fall?" I asked. "Wasn't your spotter paying attention?"

"Oh, he was paying attention, all right. He bumped me on purpose. Just because I'd been talking to another seps. Oh, the other one was so *kee-yute*! But my spotter thought I was his personal property or something and shouldn't talk to anyone else."

"Who was your spotter?" Mimi asked.

"That boy Kim likes," Darci reported, and then turned to look at me. "You know. Earl."

"Earl?" Mimi asked.

Earl, I repeated silently as all hope faded. Attending school with Earl Spikes was even worse than being on the *Bulletin* staff with Ashlee Brinkerhoff. "You don't mean Earl Spikes!" I said out loud.

"Yes. The boy we saw at the ZCMI snack bar last month. You should have seen how awful he acted in my gym class. Pushing people, and swearing at them, and making me fall. Not to mention the fact that he's the ugliest boy in the whole school. I don't know what you see in him. His teeth are brown, and his breath smells like pig slop. I think he chews tobacco or something."

"No, I don't think he *chews* tobacco," I said. "But all the kids in his family smoke pipes." I winced, remembering the smell.

"There you go defending him. Pipes don't turn your teeth *that* brown. I can't understand how you could defend him after he deliberately knocked me down."

Mimi grinned. She remembered as well as I did

how horrible the Spikeses had been; how they'd smoked eye-watering pipe tobacco and stored cut-up worms in Mrs. Overfield's crystal candy dish and tried to sell her genuine seventeenth-century jade Buddha at a cheap antique store in Park City.

"I wasn't defending him," I argued.

"Yes, you were," Darci said. "Just because you think he's kee-yute."

"I don't think Earl Spikes is cute! I never said that! You did!" Someone was yelling. Me?

Darci puckered her face; it looked like the face of one of those dried-apple dolls. "I'm only repeating what you told me yourself. You told me that on a scale of one to ten you thought he was at least a seven."

Mimi choked, trying to hold back a laugh. At least she wasn't crying anymore.

Yelling was getting me nowhere. I lowered my voice. "Earl Spikes doesn't even go to Bryant." I took a deep breath. "Does he?"

Darci sat up and calmly rearranged her ice bags and pillows and boxes of tissues. "Yes. Earl and his sister both. Until Mrs. Marler kicks them out. The principal at Murray Junior High made Earl repeat seventh grade two years ago. This year he had the choice of repeating eighth grade at Murray or transferring to another school. He and the principal both decided that it would be better if he transferred to another school, so he and his sister chose Bryant. Can you believe that?"

I could believe that Murray's principal had wanted to get rid of Earl. What I couldn't believe was that Earl and DeVeda had chosen any school at all. If they'd registered at Bryant this morning, it could only be because they'd been chauffeured there by a truant officer in a locked patrol car with a snarling dog from the K–9 corps guarding them the entire way.

Darci leaned up on an elbow to plump her pillow. "I'm sure you'll get over your crush on him when you get to know him as well as I do, Kim. He's a total mafia type. He came over while I was lying on the floor with my leg broken in two places and shook his fist at me and told me not to talk to that other seps again. It was awful. The only way I could calm him down was to tell you said he was *kee-yute.*"

Mimi's face turned red. She bent over to grab her stomach. You didn't have to be a $200-an-hour psychic to figure out why. Because she was laughing her fool head off, that's why.

I felt my face turn red, too, but I wasn't exactly laughing. A few hours earlier, when Mrs. Paddock had told me that Ashlee Brinkerhoff was going to be the *Bryant Bulletin* editor, I had thought that nothing worse could ever happen to me. But now I'd discovered that it had. Not only would Earl and DeVeda be sneaking through the halls of my very own school, but Darci Decker, my so-called friend, had told Earl Spikes—that slimy polecat, that underage degenerate, that red-haired escapee from a monster factory—that I thought he was *kee-yute.*

"I can't believe Ashlee's nerve," Darci was saying.

I'd lost track of the conversation between Darci and Mimi while I'd been worrying about meeting The Monster and his sister face-to-face at school.

"She barged right into my bedroom and asked to try it on," Darci continued, nodding toward her red-and-gray cheerleading outfit, which was hanging on the closet door. "And when it fit her, she offered to pay me one-third of what I'd paid for it— *one-third!*—if she gets on the squad. I can't stand the thought of going to the football and basketball games and seeing her in my uniform."

"Think how *I'll* feel if she ends up as my partner," Mimi commiserated. "How would you like to have Ashlee climbing all over your shoulders?"

"That's what she's going to do to me on the newspaper staff," I interrupted. "Ashlee's the new *Bulletin* editor."

"Are you sure?" Darci asked.

I nodded. "Mrs. Paddock told me they'd chosen

Ashlee for editor and me for associate editor."

"I can't believe that," Darci said. "You dropped out of cheerleading tryouts so you could be the editor! You'd make a much better editor than Ashlee."

I shrugged.

"It isn't fair! What right does she have to take the positions that both of us want?" Darci complained.

Before we could figure out how to deal with all the unfair things in life, Mrs. Decker came into Darci's room leading another visitor—my mother.

Mama was carrying a balloon bouquet for Darci and a lemon meringue pie from Marie Callender's, which she knew was Darci's favorite. Of course she wanted to hear about Darci's accident. When she found out the Spikes kids had transferred to Bryant, I thought she was going to have a stroke.

"With Mrs. Overfield on that Fun Bus to Las Vegas!" she exclaimed. "What if those children should find that out?"

"Well," I said, "at least you had the locks changed on the doors and told Mrs. Overfield to hide her car in the parking lot by the Greyhound Bus depot. How did you know about Darci's accident, anyway?"

"Miss Hudson told me."

"Miss Hudson?" I repeated.

"The cheerleading coach. Isn't that her name?

She called to tell you that she was going to hold tryouts again on Thursday for all the girls who made the first cut last spring. She said that she knew that you were going to be the associate editor of the newspaper. But the editor of the paper—Ashlee Brinkerhoff—had asked if she could try out again, so Miss Hudson thought it was only fair to invite you, too."

"Great!" Darci turned to me. "If she beat you for the paper, you can beat her for the cheerleading squad."

"Everyone on the team would rather have you than Ashlee," Mimi added. "Brynne and Jannalee really felt bad when you dropped out of tryouts last spring."

Darci looked at the pleated red skirt and the gray top hanging from her door. "I'd much rather have you wear my cheerleading outfit."

"What if I can't beat her?"

"You can," said Darci, "if you try hard enough."

"Darci and I will coach you," said Mimi. "Please?"

I took a deep breath. What did I have to lose? "Okay."

"Kiss that girl!" said Darci.

Mimi did.

So did Mama.

Darci sat up and kissed me, too.

7

"Oh, no!" Mimi covered her face with her hands. "No *what?*" I asked.

It was Thursday after school, and Mimi and I had just entered the gym for cheerleading tryouts, the first of two rounds. Already my stomach felt like a swarm of gnats, so I was in no mood to have her fall apart on me.

Still hiding her face, Mimi pointed with a bony elbow. "By the judges' table. Oh, I can't stand it if they see me."

I looked, but all I saw were the five teenage girls sitting at the table, probably cheerleaders from East or West or Highland High School, who had been hauled in to do the judging. They scared the heebie-jeebies out of me, of course, but they shouldn't have thrown Mimi into a panic.

"The judges?" I said.

"No. Behind them."

I looked again. Ernie Crenshaw was strutting back and forth in a clean white dress shirt and light tan trousers, looking as stiff and tidy as a brand-new pocket protector. I figured he'd come to the girls' cheerleading tryouts because he was still pining about the cancellation of the Welcome Day assembly and needed an official school function to preside over.

"You don't mean Earnest Ernest?"

"Of course not," Mimi said with a groan. "Sitting in the stands. It's Ashlee with those four boys we saw last Monday, the ones in the convertible who, like, called me names. Another girl is with them, too. Are they looking at me?"

"Ashlee's friends? No. They probably won't even recognize you. You're wearing jeans now."

"But what if they do recognize me?" She spread her fingers apart to peek for herself.

"Why should you care? You're a cheerleader, aren't you? Cheerleaders are supposed to be looked at. Hey! Darci's here with Brynne and Jannalee. She must have got her cast on today. Let's go sit with them."

I tugged Mimi's arm in the direction of where our friends were sitting, but before we got there, all four of those depraved Spikeses came parading into the gym. And the worry about what they might be doing here turned the swarming gnats in my stomach to frantic bees. So far I'd been lucky enough to avoid Earl and DeVeda Spikes in the halls of Bryant Junior High, but now I was suddenly face-to-face with not only those two but Calvin and Bubba Joe besides.

I'd forgotten how much the Spikes kids resembled one another, like clones from a test tube that had somehow grown at different rates of speed. But the frizzy hair—the color of fresh carrots—and the freckles—so thick their faces were orange, too—were exactly as I remembered them in my nightmares.

They approached Mimi and me in order of size and age, Earl first. He skulked past, his long arms hanging nearly to his knees and his eyes looking straight ahead, as if Mimi and I didn't exist. Next came DeVeda, not saying a word but staring at us so craftily with her slitty green eyes that for an instant I was worried that she might really have that IQ of 146 she was always bragging about. After DeVeda came Calvin, who'd always seemed the most reasonable of the bunch and I guess my favorite—if it were possible to have a favorite among the marauding Huns who'd come to rob you blind of everything that wasn't bolted to the floor. Last came Bubba Joe, the youngest and smallest of the tribe but the most dangerous. I knew from personal experience that Bubba Joe's toes felt like reinforced concrete. One kick to your shins and you'd be crippled in half a second flat.

"How's Thomas Jefferson?" Calvin asked me. I was sure he was referring to Mrs. Overfield's cat, not the president of the United States.

"Uh, just fine," I said. "You did a good job of training him. He's the first cat I ever met who comes when people call."

"I tried to phone Mrs. Over—I mean Aunt Gloria— to ask about him, but no one answered." For a minute Calvin had forgotten that the Spikeses had tried to pose as Mrs. Overfield's relatives.

"Well, don't bother to call again. Mrs. Overfield has gone to Las Vegas on a Fun Bus," Mimi said.

Cripes! I couldn't believe what she was saying, knowing what she did about the Spikeses and what they could do to an unoccupied house. For a girl who gets straight A's in every subject, Mimi Saltzgiver is thicker than a retaining wall.

All four pairs of Spikes eyes turned to focus on Mimi, even Earl's.

"How long will she be gone?" DeVeda asked sweetly.

"Oh, she should be back at any minute now," I said.

Mimi suddenly realized her mistake. "And even if she isn't, she had all her locks changed before she left."

"Where's her car?" Earl wanted to know.

"Not in our garage," I answered.

"Not anywhere you'd think to look," Mimi said.

DeVeda was unfazed. Her voice could have sweetened vinegar. "The Fun Bus is part of the Greyhound line, isn't it?"

"No, I don't think so," I lied. "Anyhow, I think maybe she and her friends chartered one of those limos you see advertised on TV."

Bubba Joe frowned. DeVeda whispered something to Earl.

But Calvin had something else on his mind. He grinned at me. "We came to help you be a cheerleader! Isn't that right, Bubba Joe?"

"Glmmp, glmmp," said Bubba Joe. He was chewing a big wad of something. Two big wads of something. Both his cheeks poked out like a chipmunk's.

"Huh?" I said.

"DeVeda says the person who gets the loudest clapping always wins. So we came to clap for you," Calvin explained.

"Hey, that's great!" said Mimi.

I wanted to punch her. I also wanted to tell the Spikeses that the only way they could help me was to leave the gym right that minute, before Miss Hudson or the judges or anyone at Bryant Junior High School found out that I knew them and held me guilty for whatever felonies they were planning to commit. But I knew if I put up any kind of resistance, they'd just be all the more obnoxious and humiliating. "That's nice," I said, lying for the second time in less than a minute.

"DeVeda says we can't clap for no one else," Calvin said.

"I'm glad you're here. We can really use your help," Mimi bubbled.

I shot her a dirty look, which she ignored.

"Clap as loud as you can," Mimi went on. "Just don't clap for Ashlee Brinkerhoff. She thinks she's going to win, but we don't want her to."

"Who's she?" asked DeVeda.

Mimi pointed. "That girl in the third row. The one with the big pink bow in her hair. Don't clap for her."

"We won't, will we, Bubba Joe?" Calvin elbowed his little brother.

"Glmmp, glmmp," said Bubba Joe.

"Come on now," ordered Earl, pointing. "We want dibs on them there places in the front row."

The Spikeses rushed toward the bleachers as Mimi and I walked more slowly toward our friends, who were sitting on folding chairs. I told Darci how thrilled I was that she was out of bed now and thanked my other friends for coming, too. But I had a hard time sitting still. I was more scared than I cared to admit about going head-to-head with Ashlee Brinkerhoff in another competition.

I took off my backpack. Then I stood up and wiped my sweaty hands against the sides of my shorts, trying not to think about Ashlee, or the groupies who'd come to root for her, or the embarrassing scenes the Spikeses might make, or anything but the routine I'd worked up for the tryouts.

Thirteen girls who had made the first cut for the cheerleading tryouts last spring had been invited back to compete again. Most of them were clustered near Miss Hudson, no doubt asking for information that hadn't already been covered in the cheerleading packets last May or the handouts she'd given to us earlier in the week. I decided that I should join them.

At six feet two, Miss Hudson towered over all of the cheerleading hopefuls. Her short, wispy hair grew every which way, like wheat in a windstorm. Her shoulders were the size of a loveseat. Her hips, narrow as a boy's, fit snugly into designer jeans that ended just above her state-of-the-art Reeboks. From the rear she could have been an NFL quarterback.

"Do I have to do a Herkie?" a girl was whining.

"Herkies are easy. I don't want to do a banana," another girl complained.

I figured neither girl had ever taken a class from Miss Hudson or heard any of the stories about her that circulated in the halls. The rest of us held our breaths while we waited for the coach to answer.

Miss Hudson squinted. "No one has to do any jumps." She widened her nostrils and stuck out her lower jaw. "They can get their sissy behinds out of my gym right this minute."

The first girl gasped out loud. The second took a half-step backward.

No one else dared to speak.

"Any more questions?" Miss Hudson asked.

The gym became so silent that you could hear Earnest Ernest cracking his knuckles. "All right then, soldiers," she said mildly. "All of you sit down on the bleachers and wait for your names to be called. When you hear your name, snap it up to the table pronto and give the judges your permission slip. Give Ernie Crenshaw copies of your yell. He'll distribute them to the audience."

On hearing his name, Earnest Ernest stood up

and bowed stiffly. He had to be loving this. I figured it was the most important assignment he'd been given since he was the chalkboard monitor in first grade.

"Remember," Miss Hudson continued, "you have to demonstrate two yells, a familiar school yell and a new one you've made up. If your yells don't include them, you must show us the four jumps on the handout plus a high kick. Extra points for a backflip and the splits. Got it? All right, soldiers. Places." *Ooo-eee!* went her whistle.

I felt my heart pounding as I went back to my seat, again wiping my hands on the sides of my shorts. How could my hands be so wet when my mouth felt so dry? I wondered if the girls Miss Hudson had chewed out felt half as scared as I did.

As the first six contestants went through their routines, I began to feel a little better. All of them were sloppy with their fists and blades. Only one girl could do the splits, and no one even attempted a backflip. Maybe I could make the squad after all.

Then Miss Hudson called out another name. "Ashlee Brinkerhoff!"

There were whistles and hoots all over the room as Ashlee stood up in her pleated pink miniskirt and tight-fitting sweater. You had to admit that she had the kind of shape that interests boys—sort of like a dainty little chest of drawers with the top drawer pulled all the way out. Every immature male in the audience was whooping his appreciation.

Ashlee's L.A. Gears were blinding white. Her spotless ankle socks poked out of her shoes in perfect little ruffles. Her long black hair was pulled back with a crisp pink bow. I couldn't help looking down at my white shorts, which had been brand-new and neatly pressed half an hour ago. Now they looked like bed sheets that had been slept in beyond the Board of Health's legal limit.

Ashlee flashed a toothy smile at her admirers around the room, sent them a delicate wave, and pranced toward the judges' table to check in. Faster than you could blink, Earl Spikes shot out one of his rubber-thonged feet in her path and Ashlee went sprawling to the floor. *Thud!*

Earnest Ernest happened to be walking to the judges' table at exactly the same minute, so everyone thought he'd knocked Ashlee down. Even he did.

"Oh, I'm so sorry," he said. "Please forgive me. Are you all right?"

Ashlee nodded bravely, but she didn't look quite as adorable as she had a few moments earlier. Her hair ribbon was a bit lopsided and both her knees were skinned. She rested for a minute on the floor and then allowed Ernie to pull her to her feet. But the fall only made the audience love her more, and her groupies led everyone else in a round of applause. Ashlee took the copies of her yell to the judges' table and then trotted back to the center of the room, waving prettily to the crowd.

I saw DeVeda frown and then lean over to whisper in Bubba Joe's ear as Ashlee began her routine.

She began with a kick—so fast and so high that she could have broken her own nose.

The audience clapped.

Next she demonstrated three jumps: Spread-eagle. Herkie. Banana.

The crowd clapped harder.

Then she performed optionals: Front splits. Side splits. A backflip.

The crowd roared. She could do no wrong. Except to a few of us, who weren't fooled.

When she led us in the most familiar Bryant yell,

> B-B-B-R-Y–A-A-A-N-T
> B-R-Y–A-N-T
> Bryant

she ended with a great toe touch. But I'd been watching her upper body work and knew it was sloppy. Her fingers came apart, her wrists went limp, and her arm angles didn't stay in line.

Mimi tapped me on the shoulder. "Did you see how, like, ragged she was? Did you see?"

"Like turkey feathers," Darci agreed.

I nodded, but I wondered if the judges had noticed.

Finally, Earnest Ernest handed out the instructions for Ashlee's original yell. When people saw how the copies had been printed up—with cutesy full-color graphics—ripples of enthusiasm spread through the gym. It hardly seemed to matter that Ashlee's arm movements still weren't precise as she led us through the yell. I knew that the judges would be listening to the crowd's response as part of their rating. And the crowd, at least the guys in it, loved her. The kids who had been sitting with her even gave her a standing ovation, and a few other people joined in.

The thunderous applause seemed to infuriate Bubba Joe. He looked behind him at Ashlee's friends, who were clapping madly, then sprang to his feet and trotted over to the judges' table, where Ashlee had gone to bestow her smiles and personal charm on the five girls sitting there. Looking straight at her, Bubba Joe puffed out his cheeks even farther. Then suddenly the wads of brown tobacco he'd been chewing sailed into the air.

Ashlee saw what was coming and ducked just in time. Some of the brown spittle landed on the judges' papers and maybe even on the judges themselves, considering the way they reacted. They shrieked and hollered, scattering like a flock of magpies in the path of a speeding train. But it was poor Ernie Crenshaw—his starched white shirt, to be precise—that caught the biggest clumps of yuck. For the second time in less than five minutes it was just his bad luck to be standing in exactly the wrong place at exactly the wrong time.

The audience howled with laughter. Earnest Ernest rubbed his eyes as if he might cry. Bubba Joe grinned.

Ooo-eee! went Miss Hudson's whistle, and the crowd went silent as she caught Bubba Joe by the ear and yanked him to the center of the room.

"Okay, soldiers. We're going to take a half-hour break while the judges try to recoup their scores for the first seven contestants and this young man cleans up his mess. Be back here at exactly"—Miss Hudson looked at the wall clock and then in Darci's direction—"four-twenty. Anyone on crutches can stay here for the break, but the rest of you soldiers get out of here. Now!"

8

At least the break gave me a chance to get a drink of water. My mouth felt dry as lint from a clothes dryer. As other people headed toward the rest rooms or the new computer games in the library, I went to the drinking fountain in the hall for a long swig. Ah!

Behind me someone spoke. "You love him, don't you?"

I whipped around. "Huh?"

DeVeda's eyes, two slits the color of peppermint mouthwash, were staring at me so hard the muscles just under my left eye started doing a strange dance. Twitch. Twitch. Twitch.

"You love Earl, don't you?" DeVeda's right hand was balled into a fist.

I looked from DeVeda's fist to the back of Earl's

neck, so thick it must have been twice the size of his IQ. He was standing about twelve feet away, studying his right foot as he tried to screw the sole of his drugstore thong into the linoleum.

"Well, no, I—"

"Don't lie. Your friend Darci told him all about it."

My *friend* Darci? At that moment I wouldn't have cared if Earl had broken both her legs.

"It's all right," DeVeda said. "He loves you, too. He says you and him is going to be the king and queen of the fall dance. You and him is going to make a very romantic couple. Soon as you get on the cheerleading squad and he gets on the football team, you can run for king and queen. You'll win, too. Him and me know all about winning elections. We got him elected student body president at Murray last spring, and he would have been a good one, too, if that stupid principal hadn't been such a diddlehead."

Somehow I recovered my voice. "I don't want to be the fall queen."

DeVeda stepped so close that I could smell the tortilla chips and extra-hot salsa she'd been eating. Her eyes narrowed to even thinner slits. "Yes, you do," she said menacingly. "You want exactly what Earl and me say."

Once upon a time—it seemed a million years

ago—I had thought that the Spikeses might be afraid of me. Now I knew that had never been true.

Holding my breath, I took a step backward. What would the Spikeses do if I refused? Break my legs plus my arms, too? Those things would hurt, of course, but I'd recover in a few months. But being the fall queen with Earl Spikes was a humiliation that would last my whole life.

"I'm not eligible," I said. "Only cheerleaders can run for fall queen, and I won't make the cheerleading squad. Did you see Ashlee Brinkerhoff just now? She got a standing ovation. The judges will be sure to choose someone who gets a standing ovation, and I can never do that."

For an instant DeVeda bit her lip, saying nothing. Then she brightened. "Me and Earl can fix the cheerleading squad, too. You wait here and do what you're supposed to. I'll be right back."

She ran over to Earl, grabbed him by the arm, and whispered in his ear. Then together they raced down the hall. As I watched them disappear, I couldn't help wondering if I shouldn't beat it out of this place, too.

Someone slugged me on the back.

"Well, come on!" said Mimi. "We don't have much time."

"Come on *where?*"

"To Red's, of course. Help me remember. Darci wants a large cup of nonfat vanilla mixed with, like, coconut, peanut M and M's, fresh peach, malt balls, and Heath Bar."

Darci and Mimi and I had exactly the same philosophy about frozen yogurt. Anything as healthy as nonfat vanilla would cancel out all the calories and saturated fat in anything else the counter guys at Red's mixed with it. And we loved inventing new combinations. But right then my stomach was too jumpy for food. I didn't want anything stronger than water.

"No thanks," I said. "I'm not hungry."

"Well, Darci and I are famished. She can't walk that far, and I don't want to go alone. Come *on!*"

"All right," I said. I might as well keep her company since the only other thing I had to do was stay here and worry.

I grabbed my backpack and trotted along to keep up with Mimi's long strides—down the hall, out the door, across the street, and into the sweet-smelling interior of Red's Frozen Yogurt.

The counter girl was all alone in the store, so I expected her to say something like "Hi" or "Nice day, isn't it?" or "What can I get you?" which is what salespeople do when they have too much time on their hands. But she didn't. "Do you know any redheaded kids?"

I must have stopped in my tracks. "Well—" I said.

I was sure she was going to tell us that a boy and a girl with carroty-red hair and freckles like orange gumballs had just robbed her safe of the whole week's take. They'd even told her why they needed the cash—for bribe money to make sure the judges of the cheerleading tryouts at Bryant chose the girl they wanted to win. Not many bandits would be dumb enough to make a remark like that, which would be a sure tip-off to the police. But you could never tell about the Spikeses.

The girl's head swept in a circle, indicating the pictures of all the redheaded kids on the walls. "We're going to redecorate. Get pictures of new kids to display. So we're having a contest to find eight photogenic redheads under the age of thirteen. It's a great contest. We'll make the winners famous—we'll hang framed twenty-four- by thirty-six-inch pictures of them in every Red's store in the city. And each of their mothers gets a complete beauty makeover plus a two-hundred-dollar gift certificate at Nordstrom."

She was so nice that I figured I should make conversation with her even though I couldn't think of any redheads besides the obnoxious Spikeses.

"How do you apply?" I said.

"Just fill out those entry forms." She nodded toward the stack of them on her counter. "One for each entrant. But you've got to hurry. The winners will be chosen next Monday."

While Mimi ordered two of the famous Mimi Saltzgiver–Darci Decker frozen-yogurt inventions for herself and Darci, I sat down at one of the tables and read an entry form. My eyes nearly popped out when I discovered that the contestants and their mothers all had to be present for the judging next Monday afternoon. Monday afternoon—the very same time that the cheerleading finals would be going on at Bryant. If the Spikeses were at the Red's judging, they couldn't be present to humiliate me at the cheerleading tryouts. Even the Spikeses couldn't manage to be in two places at the same time.

It would be easier to drag a mule toward a vet holding a giant syringe than it would be to get the Spikes kids to show up for a contest like this. But I'd be willing to bet my entire CD collection that Mrs. Spikes was just the sort of mother who'd try. From what I'd seen of her (only one peek from behind a plant in ZCMI), it was my guess that if any of her kids knew how to tap-dance or whistle or juggle as many as two tennis balls, she would have marched them straight to a talent agent on their third birthdays. And she would have done it even without the promise of a complete beauty make-over and a two-hundred-dollar gift certificate for herself.

It was worth a shot. I picked up three more applications and started filling them out.

I didn't know the exact ages for any of the kids, much less their address and phone number and mother's name. But I have to admit I had fun listing their hobbies and talents:

EARL SPIKES: elected student body president at Murray Junior High; planning to be a member of the Bryant Junior High football team; planning to be the king of the fall dance; huge muscles that he uses to protect his little sister and brothers from nosy neighbors; occasional spotter for girls' gymnastics.

DEVEDA SPIKES: campaign manager for her brother Earl and any other people Earl thinks should win something; future race-car driver; original thinker and planner; IQ of 146.

CALVIN SPIKES: famous cat trainer (house variety); shoe model for Nike, Adidas, L.A. Gear, Reebok, and British Knights; future botanist (takes very good care of exotic houseplants such as Venus's-flytraps).

BUBBA JOE SPIKES: future placekicker for the NFL (toes are stronger than a Russian tank) or shortstop for the American League (has a special talent for spitting) or linguist (uses words that haven't even been invented yet).

I was smiling proudly at my cleverly answered entry forms when Mimi walked over, swirling her tongue around the top of her frozen-yogurt mixture.

"What are you doing?" she asked.

"I'm keeping the Spikeses away from tryouts on Monday. See?" I said, handing her the forms.

She grinned as she read them. Then her expression changed. "This won't work. It says right here that the owner of Red's is going to telephone the mothers of the contestants to get their permission and tell them where the judging will take place. You know they have an unlisted number. We spent all summer trying to find it."

"Yeah, but I have a better incentive now. And I still have four days until Monday." With that, I folded the applications neatly and put them in my backpack.

9

The minute Mimi and I walked back inside the school, I remembered my last conversation there with DeVeda. She'd promised that she could fix things so I'd get on the cheerleading squad, and whatever her plans were, I was sure they wouldn't be legal. The question was, would she get only herself and Earl expelled or would I get kicked out of Bryant, too?

Mimi and I walked into the gym and gave Darci her frozen yogurt. Darci and Mimi joked about how Miss Hudson had made Bubba Joe clean up his mess during the break in the cheerleading tryouts and how Ernie Crenshaw had called his mother to come take him home. But I felt kind of sorry for Earnest Ernest and was too nervous to enjoy the humor. I sat down on the bleachers and watched silently while the rest of the contestants went through their routines.

My stomach rolled like a waterbed. My ears pounded like two bass drums. My eyes were so blurry, I could have been watching the performances of the rest of the cheerleading wanna-bes through a sixty-gallon tank of kelpy brine.

"Kim Sanders," said a faraway voice.

"Kim Sanders," the voice repeated louder.

"Kim Sanders!"

Darci poked me. "Go on."

"Huh?"

"It's your turn."

Like a robot with a half-dead battery, I gathered up my papers, walked over to the table, and handed the judges my permission slip. Then I gave the copies of my original yell to Ernie's replacement and faced the audience.

I suppose my body had spent so many hours practicing all of the arm signals and body movements Mimi and Darci had taught me that it didn't even need my brain. Don't ask me how I did it, but somehow I got through all the routines I'd been working on—kicks, jumps, splits, backflips, even two complete Bryant Junior High School yells.

The applause woke me up. Actually, it wasn't exactly applause—it was more like hooting and stamping and whistling and drumming and all sorts of ear-splitting noise. And it was coming from the section of the bleachers where all the Spikes kids were standing and banging on the homemade instruments DeVeda had rounded up—kitchen pans and wooden blocks and a pair of wheezy harmonicas. DeVeda turned around to signal the rest of the audience to join in the uproar and a few people did, including one of the teenage boys who had started the applause for Ashlee. Pretty soon nearly half the people in the room were on their feet in a standing ovation. For me.

I'd never had a standing ovation before, especially one that noisy, so for half a second I was almost proud. But then that gang of Spikes dingbats kicked off their thongs to stage a barefoot "Kim Sanders" procession around the gym. Pounding a kitchen pan with a big spoon and prancing on her grimy toes, DeVeda took the lead. Next came Earl, clapping two huge wooden blocks together. Last came Calvin and Bubba Joe, blowing the same notes in and out on their rusty-sounding harmonicas and carrying a red-and-black banner printed with lopsided letters: WE ❤ KIM. In rhythm with the harmonicas, DeVeda and Earl chanted "SAN-ders, SAN-ders, SAN-ders" until nearly the whole audience joined in.

My cheeks grew hot. I wanted to duck under the bleachers and evaporate. I wanted to fly to Alaska and live in an igloo. I wanted to join one of those FBI witness-protection programs where they change your name and your fingerprints and hide you in another part of the world for the rest of your natural life.

Suddenly, one of the boys who was sitting with Ashlee kicked off his shoes and chased after the demonstrators. Dancing behind the Spikeses, he waved his arms and wiggled his hips in rhythm with the chant.

Ashlee popped up faster than a jack-in-the-box, her hands clenched tightly at her sides. She raced after her friend, grabbed fistfuls of his shirt, and practically ripped it off his back.

It's hard to believe the four Spikes kids didn't notice what was going on right behind them, but they didn't. They kept right on pounding and prancing and blowing like high school band members leading a parade down Main Street on the Fourth of July. Not Ashlee's friend, though. When she yanked on his shirt, he spun around and scowled at her as if she were a dead horse covered with maggots.

With all the noise the Spikeses were making, you couldn't exactly hear what Ashlee and the boy were saying to each other. But you knew it wasn't polite conversation about the weather. She pulled off the bracelet she was wearing and threw it on the floor. Then she turned around and charged in the other direction. Toward me.

Uh-oh. I braced myself.

Ashlee stuck her nose almost against mine. Her nostrils flared. Her lips snarled. "You may think you're going to be on the cheerleading squad, but you're not. I can beat you any day of the week."

"Look, Ashlee. Something has come up. I'm not sure I even want to be a cheerleader anymore. Why don't we make a deal? I'll drop out of the cheerleading tryouts if you'll resign from the newspaper."

"Oh, yeah?" she said, and I felt little drops of spit on my face. "No way. You're just chickening out because you know I'm going to beat you. Well, I'm going to be the *Bulletin* editor and a cheerleader, too."

Over Ashlee's shoulder I could see Miss Hudson striding toward the dancing and drumming Spikes gang. *Ooo-eee!* went her whistle. "Cut that out!" she yelled.

DeVeda ended her band-majorette impression. Earl lowered the wooden blocks to his sides. Calvin stopped tooting his harmonica and dropped his side of the banner to the floor. Only Bubba Joe was unfazed by Miss Hudson's command. Maybe he didn't hear her. Maybe he didn't think she was talking to him. He stamped his foot and yelled at his brothers and sister to continue their parade. Maybe he was planning to run over and kick all of them in the shins until they started up again.

Miss Hudson clapped her enormous hand on Bubba Joe's head, squashing him so hard that he collapsed to the floor like a cardboard box under the foot of an elephant. I could hardly believe my eyes. Or my ears either. The gym fell so silent that you could hear Bubba Joe panting.

"Sit down!" Miss Hudson ordered the other Spikeses, and they did. Right on the floor by Bubba Joe.

Then she turned her steely gray eyes on *me.* Her voice was low and raspy. She was a rattler ready to strike. "There will be no more demonstrations in my gym. You see to it that your friends here behave or you'll be disqualified. Hear?"

I heard. "Yes, ma'am."

She took a deep breath and then spoke in her normal voice. "All right then, soldiers. All thirteen contestants have now performed their routines. We'll give the judges a few minutes to add up the scores and then I'll announce the six finalists.

They'll come back again next Monday after school to go through their routines a second time for a different set of judges. The names of the winner and two alternates will be announced over the loudspeaker on Tuesday."

Little by little, people started whispering again until the room droned softly. No talking, really, but lots of foot shuffling and coughing and moving back and forth until the bleachers creaked. I fidgeted, trying to make up my mind. Did I want to hang around long enough to find out who the finalists were or beat it out of here before the Spikes numskulls did something so terrible that Miss Hudson would disqualify me from every single school activity for the rest of my life?

The judges had less trouble making up their minds than I did, because a few minutes later Miss Hudson blew her whistle again and announced the finalists. Ashlee Brinkerhoff was one of them.

So was I.

Ashlee's friends, except for the boy she'd fought with, whooped and cheered. Mimi, Brynne, and Jannalee rushed over to hug me and more kids followed. Even Darci hobbled over on her brand-new crutches.

Maybe I should have been happy about all of it, but I wasn't. Now I was one step closer to being chosen queen of the fall dance with Earl Spikes. Or getting expelled from Bryant Junior High. Or being so humiliated by those pimple-brained Spikes kids that I would never dare to stick my face inside the door of this school again.

Sure enough, the four Spikeses jumped to their feet and rushed over to join the throng of kids now gathered around me.

Bubba Joe grinned. "We done good, didn't we?"

"We're going to fix it so's you'll win on Monday, too," said Calvin. "You'll be the new cheerleader."

"DeVeda has it all figured out," Bubba Joe added.

I wiped my forehead with the back of my hand. "Uh, listen, DeVeda," I stammered, "I don't think it's a very good idea for you kids to come back on Monday. You could get me disqualified." I leaned toward her, begging. "Please. I'm not sure I even want to be a cheerleader."

DeVeda hunched her shoulders and stared back at me with her slitty eyes. "Yes, you do," she whispered back. "Remember?"

For the first time since he'd transferred to Bryant, Earl spoke directly to me. He elbowed me and winked. "Remember?"

That seemed to be a cue for Bubba Joe. He pointed to Earl and me and spoke loudly enough for everyone nearby to hear: "Him and her wants to be king and queen of the fall dance together."

Mouths fell open. Eyes widened. Darci shook her head with pity. Mimi tried to stifle a grin.

"No!" I cried. "We don't!"

DeVeda stitched her mouth together with an invisible drawstring. Calvin chewed his lip. Earl rammed his hands in his pockets and studied the floor. Bubba Joe lowered his head and scowled up at me, the way he does just before he's ready to kick someone.

Even though I'd personally been kicked a couple of times last summer by Bubba Joe's cast-iron toes and suspected they could put you in a wheelchair for the rest of your natural life, I had to make sure that everyone around us understood the exact truth. I took a deep breath and then spoke slowly. "Earl and I sort of lived next door to each other once, but it wasn't for very long, and we hardly even spoke to each other the whole time."

It was too late. Three girls were already pointing at Earl and me and grinning like a family of chimpanzees. Other people slowly backed away as if I had some terminal disease they might catch.

"She's lying!" DeVeda hissed.

And then, as if he hadn't already made me seem nuttier than a pecan pie, Bubba Joe pointed again and shouted so loudly that Ashlee and her friends across the room stopped talking. "He's my big brother Earl. Him and her love each other."

"She says he's handsome," Calvin added for good measure.

"A perfect ten," DeVeda said smugly.

Help, I thought. *H-E-L-L-L-P!*

10

was so late getting out of fourth-period history on Friday that I didn't have time to go to my locker to get rid of my backpack. Mimi was waiting alone for me outside the cafeteria.

"Where's Darci?" I asked.

"Oh, some *kee-yute* boy offered to help her catch up with an English assignment she missed this week, so she decided she wasn't hungry. She's skipping lunch to meet him at the media center."

"Did you see him?"

"Uh-huh," Mimi said. "His fingernails looked dirty enough to grow peanuts, but you know Darci."

I knew Darci, all right. "Well, let's go eat, then. I'm starved."

Mimi made a face. "In a minute. There's something you should know first. I just saw Earl and

DeVeda Spikes opening your locker and putting something inside. Then they locked it again and sneaked off with real guilty looks on their faces."

I guess maybe my chin fell. For twenty-four hours I'd managed to stay away from those lawbreakers, and I'd hoped they might have forgotten about me.

"They couldn't open my locker unless they figured out my combination."

"Maybe they got someone to watch you do it."

"Are you sure you saw them open it?" I asked.

"Does my father hate taxes?" Mimi asked.

"Cripes!" I said, and took off like a derby winner chased by a swarm of bees. For once, long-legged Mimi tagged behind.

But when I got to within ten feet of my locker, I stopped. Maybe the Spikeses had put a dead mouse inside, the way DeVeda had done to the backpack of that girl who used to be in my geometry class. Maybe they'd done something really criminal, like wired the door to electrocute me when I opened it. Maybe they'd even planted a bomb inside to blow up the whole school. I didn't really figure they were planning to murder anyone, but you never could tell.

"Well? Aren't you going to open it?" Mimi asked.

I looked around to see how many kids might die along with me, but the hall was nearly empty. Most of them had already gone to the cafeteria. "Stand back," I told Mimi. She stepped away. "Farther."

When she'd moved about fifteen feet, I dialed the combination and opened the door gingerly. Cripes. After getting so worked up about what might be inside, it was almost disappointing to see what the Spikeses had put in my locker. Just a note on a smudged piece of lined paper. I picked it up.

The note was covered with lopsided hearts made with a red Magic Marker. Right away I knew that Earl had written it. Either that or DeVeda's off-the-chart IQ didn't extend to spelling:

My Darling,

We is going to mess up Ashlys head so she cant do nothing rite on Monday.

Hide in the girls bathroom on A coridor across the hall from Ashlys loker after scool to see the fun. It will be *grate!!!!*

Earl Spikes and Kim Sanders

Lovers Forever

P.S. Mom thinks all are freinds are a bad infloons on us. She keeps changeing are phone number so noone cant call up. Rite now its 724–3111 and you can call till it changes agin. Please, dearest. My hart is yours only.

After seeing what they'd put in my locker, I figured those redheaded nutcases wouldn't do too much to Ashlee's either. Probably just send her a stupid note, too. But what gave that egomaniac the nerve to think I'd want to call him? And how had he and DeVeda gotten the combinations to other people's lockers anyhow? I had a good mind to march to the principal's office right that minute to report them to Mrs. Marler!

Then I remembered what had happened to the girl in my geometry class. Tattling on the Spikeses might not be a very good idea. I wadded up the note into a tight ball and hurled it toward the wastebasket. I guess I was too angry to take careful aim. It landed nearly a foot short.

"You'll never make the basketball team," Mimi said, swooping down on the paper like a starving owl spotting a mouse. A polite friend would have respected my privacy. She would have picked up the paper for me and put it straight into the wastebasket. Not Mimi. She read the note. Right out loud.

"Oh, this is, like, un-*real*!" she said afterward. Then she covered her mouth with her hand, but you didn't have to have X-ray vision to know she was grinning.

I rolled my eyes.

"Earl Spikes and Kim Sanders," she said with a titter.

"Very funny," I said.

"Lovers forever," she said, laughing louder. She held the note out toward me. "Here. You'll need your lover's number."

"Joke's over," I said, but it wasn't.

"You better use it fast before his mother, like, changes it," Mimi said between guffaws.

Some friends! I thought. My supposed best friend gets me into the worst mess of my entire life, which another friend thinks is so funny she nearly bursts a kidney laughing.

But at least Mimi had given me an idea. "Thanks. I *do* need this!" I said. I snatched the note, slammed my locker shut, and charged down the hall toward the outside door, my backpack still strapped over my shoulders.

Suddenly, Mimi wasn't laughing anymore. "Hey! Where are you going?"

I didn't answer.

She sprinted after me, and even with the head-start I'd had, she caught right up. "Are you really going to, like, call him?"

I didn't answer.

"I bet you're going to call his mother. Is that it?"

I still didn't answer, but she saw where I was headed.

"Oh, I get it. It's the Red's contest. Now that you have their number, you're going to, like, enter the Spikes kids."

I finally spoke, but only through clenched teeth. "Give the comedian half a star."

"Oh, don't be such a bad sport. I bet you would have laughed if Earl had sent that note to me."

Yeah, maybe she was right.

So we made up, and she went to Red's with me and helped put the Spikeses' phone number on each of the entry forms I'd been carrying around in my backpack. For their mother's name we just wrote "Mrs. Spikes." Then we got up from our chairs and walked over to the counter.

"Make sure you have someone call the mother of these kids so they'll be at the judging next Monday," I told the counter girl. "It's really important."

"You're getting these entries in kind of late," the girl said. "I'm not sure we'll be able to reach their mother."

I leaned over the counter. "Do you know who Ernie Crenshaw is?"

"N-no."

"He's the student body president of Bryant," Mimi explained.

"The most unusual president Bryant's ever had," I added.

"So?" said the girl.

"You get lots of business from Bryant kids," I reminded her. "It would be a personal favor to our student body president if you saw to it that these Spikes children come to the judging next Monday."

"I don't see—"

"Ernie would be really grateful," I said.

"All the kids would," Mimi added.

Now that we were discussing Bryant students and their president, I remembered the campaign oratory that had persuaded voters to elect Ernie last spring. I took a deep breath and gave the counter girl my best Earnest Ernest imitation. "Everyone in this world deserves the chance to compete. The highest and noblest among us. The meekest and the humblest. All of us deserve the chance to throw our hats into the ring. To stand up and be counted. To put our shoulders to the wheel."

"To keep our eyes on the stars," Mimi chimed in. "To put our nose to the grindstone. To juggle our opportunities."

"To catch the ball and run with it." I paused, giving emphasis to the stirring wrap-up. "To give our hands and hearts and souls to mankind."

"Huh?" The counter girl had turned cross-eyed. I couldn't tell if she were dazzled by the Crenshaw wisdom or merely falling asleep.

"We just expect your contest to be fair," I explained in simple English. "The Spikes children are getting their entries in before the deadline. They deserve the right to enter your contest."

"Ernest Crenshaw and everyone at Bryant would be, like, really grateful if you'd let them," Mimi added. "What do you have to lose?"

I picked up an application and read the girl the Spikeses' phone number.

"Well . . ." she said, and headed toward the telephone.

When her back was turned, I raised my hand for a high-five. Mimi winked at me as she smacked it.

We got back to Bryant just as the bell rang for the fifth period.

"I'll see you after school in the girls' bathroom," I told Mimi.

"What for?" she asked.

"You know. To see what Earl and DeVeda put in Ashlee's locker. You said you could walk home with me," I reminded her. The cheerleading practices had been canceled until the new girl was chosen.

"Yes, but I've got to go to the media center after school to get, like, a book for my English assignment."

"Okay," I said. "I'll look for you there after the excitement at Ashlee's locker is over."

"Watch carefully so you can tell me all about it."

I made a face. "You probably won't miss much. Just another misspelled note."

But I was wrong about that.

11

After school the A corridor was abuzz with kids shouting and lockers slamming and general T.G.I.F. excitement. Ashlee Brinkerhoff was nowhere in sight, so I headed straight to the girls' bathroom.

DeVeda's head popped out of the door. "Where have you been?" she demanded. "Me and Earl is doing all this for you, you know."

"Listen, DeVeda, I—"

"Shh," she ordered, poking my arm with a sharp elbow. "Here she comes."

Sure enough, just behind Earnest Ernest, who marched steadfastly to his own locker, Ashlee Brinkerhoff strutted down the hall in a pair of blue shorts which were still crisp after a full day at school. She paused long enough to swish her beautiful black hair and cast a honeyed smile to the adoring fans nearby. Daintily she bent over to spin the combination lock and open the door of her locker.

BAM! The explosion was so loud, it rattled my eardrums. A cloud of yellow smoke billowed from Ashlee's locker, stinking up the hall with the worst smell you could imagine—something between sewer gas and the odor you get from the Great Salt Lake about once every five years when the wind hits it just a certain way. Whoo-ee! My eyes began watering like a couple of leaky showerheads.

People coughed and sputtered and clawed their way to the exits. At the same time Ashlee grabbed Earnest Ernest by both shoulders and shook him until his hair shot out like sparks from a roman candle. *"Do something!"* she screamed. *"Are you spineless? Do something! Now!"*

Poor Ernie probably wanted to, but she was holding him so tight that he couldn't do much. The minute she let go, he scampered down the hall to smash the fire alarm, and pretty soon it began *whoo-oop*ing louder than the explosion. But by then it was too late for the alarm to be a whole lot of use. Practical-minded people had already opened all the doors and windows, so the smoke and excitement were pretty much dying down.

"Wasn't that a terrific stink bomb?" DeVeda

chirped. "I made it myself with an old battery from a dumpster and chemicals I found in the science lab. Did you see Ashlee's face when it exploded? And that was just the beginning. We have lots more things planned. She's really going to be all shook up on Monday. She won't be able to do any of those fancy jumps of hers or remember the words to that new yell she made up." Little Miss Nuclear Physicist poked me again with a flinty elbow.

I poked her right back. Two fingers straight to her forehead. "Think again, genius. Ashlee is laughing already." She was, too. People from other parts of the school had congregated in the A corridor to find out about the noise, and Ashlee was having a great time being the center of attention.

I poked DeVeda again. To the chest this time. "The only person you and Earl are upsetting with these mind games of yours is me. *I'm* the one who won't be able to do any jumps or remember the words to any yells on Monday."

DeVeda looked at Ashlee, then back at me. She pursed her lips into a fierce little knot, and for a second I thought she was planning to hit me. I wasn't too worried, though. Unless she had toes as strong as Bubba Joe's, which I doubted, she couldn't do any serious damage. She'd always been the brains of her family, not the brawn.

"Maybe you're right," she said at last. "We'll have to go straight to Plan B."

Then she whirled around and scooted toward an outside door.

With a sigh, I walked more slowly in the other direction, toward the media center, to meet Mimi, my footsteps echoing in the now-empty hall. In the distance I could hear sirens and wondered if the firemen would be steamed about rushing to an empty school to fight nothing more life-threatening than the smell of rotten eggs.

Mimi was standing at the library window. She spun around to face me as I walked into the room.

"You missed all the excitement," I said. "DeVeda set off a stink bomb in Ashlee's locker. She and Earl were trying to mess up Ashlee's head so she wouldn't win the cheerleading finals on Monday."

Mimi pointed out the window. "If Earl's so crazy about you, how come he's, like, making out with Ashlee right now?"

Sure enough, Earl seemed to be pawing Ashlee with both hands. His face was so close to hers that he was practically chewing her ear. Then they turned onto the path toward Bryant's parking lot and I could see them from a different angle.

"He isn't hugging her. He's twisting her arm behind her back."

"How come?"

"How should I know?" A hundred possibilities flashed into my mind, all so horrible that no one but the Spikeses or professional hit men from the Mafia would dare to try them.

"Look!" Mimi pointed again. "Isn't that Mrs. Overfield's car in the parking lot?"

Good night. It *was* the yellow Thunderbird. You couldn't mistake a one-in-a-million 1965 classic like that. But how had we missed seeing it at lunchtime when we'd passed the parking lot to go to Red's?

Shivers ran down my back. I was sure—I was absolutely positive—that Plan B was something far worse than stink bombs. And if people found out that it had anything to do with me, I might get expelled from school along with Earl and DeVeda. I didn't care a whole lot about what might happen to Ashlee Brinkerhoff, but I knew I had to protect her in order to save my own hide.

DeVeda was sitting in the driver's seat, her frizzy red hair barely poking above the steering wheel of the T-bird. Calvin and Bubba Joe were riding shotgun. The car was coughing and wheezing and puffing black smoke like an emphysema victim who knows he's dying but can't quite give up his smelly old cigars.

When Earl and Ashlee approached the car, Calvin climbed out the front door and opened the back one. You could tell Ashlee wasn't thrilled about where she was headed. She twisted and kicked until her huge white hair ribbon fluttered like a seagull, but Earl was stronger and managed to shove her inside the Thunderbird. Then Calvin climbed back into the front seat with Bubba Joe and DeVeda.

Vrmm. Vrmm. Screech. The car panted and spurted out of the parking lot. It was pretty obvious that DeVeda hadn't learned much about driving since last summer.

"They're kidnapping her," I muttered.

"Un-*real!*"

"Where do you think they're taking her?" I asked.

"Just a couple of blocks. To the strip mall at Fourth South and Sixth East."

"Don't joke," I said. "This is serious." Sometimes Mimi Saltzgiver made you so mad you could pound nails with your bare fists.

"I'm not joking. Earl was whispering to Calvin and Bubba Joe in the hall a few minutes ago. I heard him say something about going to that mall to get provisions."

Uh-oh. I didn't like the sound of that. *Provisions* is what Dad calls all the pots and pans and water purifiers and dehydrated food he packs up when he goes off with his fishing buddies for two or three million years.

"This could be serious," I told Mimi. "Ashlee could be in big trouble."

Mimi fanned the air with a limp hand. "Who cares? You of all people should be glad to have her, like, out of the way. With Ashlee gone, you're sure to get on the cheerleading squad. You might even get that other job you wanted—editor of the school paper."

"Look, Mimi. Things are more serious than that. If the Spikeses have stolen a car and actually kidnapped someone, they're planning something lots worse than any of the dumb things they did last summer. We could be talking federal offense here. And after that twit-headed demonstration they staged at tryouts, people might think that I'm partners with them or something. I could end up in juvenile detention, too. Or even worse."

Mimi screwed up her face, trying to decide if she agreed with me.

"Your parents are lawyers. You read lots of mystery novels," I reminded her. "You know that innocent people get blamed all the time for crimes they don't commit. And it would be just like the Spikeses to try to weasel out of trouble by putting the blame on me."

Mimi slowly nodded her head.

"We've got to stop them before they do something really terrible to Ashlee," I said. "We've got to follow them. We can't let them out of our sight."

"Un-*real*! I've always wanted to be a lady private eye. When I grow up, I'm going to be just like Kinsey Millhone. Only I plan to wear better clothes than she does. Have you read those books? She always—"

"You can tell me about it later. We need to hurry. You run to the mall right now and tail them."

"Fabulous! I won't let them out of my sight. But what are you going to do?"

"I'll come and find you just as soon as I phone my mother and tell her to meet us there with the car. If the Spikeses have a car, we'll need one, too."

"Oh, this is so exciting! When I become a private eye, I think I'll specialize in kidnappings."

12

finally located an assistant janitor willing to unlock the secretary's office long enough for me to make a telephone call to Mama.

"Listen carefully, Mom. This is important."

"Oh, hi, darling. Where are you?"

"I'm still at school. Something has happened. Mimi's waiting for both of us at the strip mall and you need to bring the car so that we can follow the Spikes kids because—"

"Hold on. My computer is printing, and I can't hear a thing."

Thunk went the receiver on the glass top of her desk. *Hmmmm* went the printer.

"Mom!" I shouted.

She didn't answer, but the computer started beeping and whining and going *ooh-ah, ooh-ah,* so I figured she was trying to turn the printer off. Mama's got one of those prehistoric Macs that take about eight years to respond to a command.

"Mom!"

"Here I am," Mama finally reported. "What were you saying?"

I gave her a fast replay of what had happened during the last hour: how DeVeda had put a stink bomb in Ashlee's locker; how Calvin and Bubba Joe had turned up at Bryant; how the Spikeses had not only committed grand theft auto on Mrs. Overfield's Thunderbird but were kidnappers besides.

"Good heavens!" Mama cried. "Don't do a thing until I get to school."

"Not Bryant, Mom. The mall. Meet us at the mall."

"Which one?"

I told her, then hung up and exited the building through the nearest door that opened onto First South.

I raced two blocks west down the street, passing helmeted teenagers jumping over curbs on their skateboards and a little kid dribbling Popsicle juice down his T-shirt and an old lady hosing squished apricots off the sidewalk.

Cripes, but it was hot, especially wearing the black nylon backpack that I'd lugged around all day. I was grateful to catch my breath for a minute while I waited for the traffic to ease up long enough for me to turn left across the street. Then I ran two more blocks south, past some kids selling lemonade from a card table and a man posting a sign that said YARD SALE SAT. 7A.M. and a house with three broken-down trucks in the driveway plus a red one parked right on the grass. It amazed me that I'd never noticed this part of town before, even though it was less than half a mile from my school.

Panting so hard my throat burned, I reached the mall and scanned the parking lot for a yellow Thunderbird. Sure enough, it was parked in plain sight, right in front of the pizza takeout. I could see one head of frizzy red hair in the backseat. Earl's.

I stopped in my tracks. Now what should I do? Look for Mimi? Wait until Mama arrived? Approach Earl while he was all alone and maybe sweet-talk him into giving me Mrs. Overfield's car keys before DeVeda returned? I looked around to make sure that DeVeda or Calvin or Bubba Joe—especially Bubba Joe—wasn't standing guard to attack me if I got too close.

Hopefully I inched forward.

"Psst! Kim!" a hoarse voice called from behind.

Who was it? I turned around. The only person I could see was a uniformed car-wash attendant. He was polishing a shiny red Vette that had just come through all those hundreds of water jets and wax sprays and dancing hula skirts.

I squinted at him.

"Over here," said the attendant, motioning.

Good night. It was Mimi. But until she'd spoken, I would have sworn she was a guy in that wild getup. A green-striped apron hung to the knees of her jeans. A green-striped cap into which she'd poked all her shoulder-length hair engulfed her head. As I walked closer, I could see two minicopies of my own face in her mirrored sunglasses.

"What's with the outfit?" I asked.

"Great, isn't it? The perfect disguise for, like, a stakeout."

You had to admit Mimi took her detective career seriously. "Where did you get it?"

She nodded toward a gangly teenage boy who was sitting on the grassy area under a tree. Lounging on one elbow, the guy was smoking a cigarette and gazing off into the clouds as if he expected to find a winning lottery number up there. "He let me borrow it if I'd do his work," Mimi explained. "But I'm going bananas trying to wipe cars and, like, watch all the doors in the mall at the same time. I'm sure glad you finally decided to get yourself here."

"I'm sorry it took so long. I had trouble finding a

way to make the phone call to Mom and—"

The driver's window rolled down and a man's blow-dried head poked out from inside the car. "Snap it up, will you? I've got to go home and change before a dinner date with a real babe."

"Yes, sir," Mimi said, just as if she were a regular kid who worked for her spending money and didn't have two lawyers for parents. She was the only friend I had who got a monthly allowance in three figures.

The window went back up, and Mimi handed me a rag. "Help me so we can talk."

I shrugged and started rubbing. "What have you found out?"

Mimi leaned my way and whispered out of the side of her mouth, "DeVeda and Calvin are in the pizza takeout. Bubba Joe's in the grocery store next door to it."

"Where's Ashlee?" I asked.

"Haven't seen her. They must have dropped her off somewhere before they got here."

I didn't know whether to be relieved about that or not. "Dropped her off" sounded ominous. Sort of like "bumped her off." But even if Ashlee was safe, the Spikes kids were still using Mrs. Overfield's car, and I knew Mama would feel responsible about that. She was the one, after all, who had gotten the brilliant idea to "hide" the Thunderbird by parking it outdoors by the Greyhound Bus depot, right in front of the entire world.

Mimi rapped on the Corvette's window. It rolled down.

"I think we're through," she said. "Do you want to inspect?"

"No time," the driver said, starting up the engine. "I trust you." He stuck his arm out the window and handed each of us a bill.

A dollar? I'd earned a whole dollar for one minute's work? That was sixty dollars an hour.

"Gee." I drew in my breath and then let it out again. "Thanks!"

Grinning, I looked at the bill in my hand. Uh-oh. My smile faded. I waved the money at the car, which was purring softly as it headed toward the street. "Hey, mister," I called. "You made a mistake! This is a five!"

"I know, I know. I figure if I'm generous with the two of you, maybe I'll get lucky tonight. Have a nice day." The window rolled up and the car turned right into the traffic lane.

My mouth fell open. I could think of a million things to do with five dollars, beginning with buying a bottle of the shampoo that the man on TV promised would make your hair look bouncy and full and shine like the gorgeous model's.

The boy who had been gazing at the heavens threw his cigarette to the street, jumped to his feet, and dashed to Mimi's side faster than you could say "Texas billionaire."

"Hey, that's mine." He grabbed for Mimi's bill.

Mimi was faster. Her hand flew behind her back. "It is not. This is the first five dollars I ever earned as a detective. I'm going to take it home and frame it and keep it on the wall for, like, the rest of my life."

"Detective!" The guy sneered. "You earned it as a car washer. Wearing *my* uniform." He reached for the money, but Mimi isn't a person who puts up with any of that male dominance stuff. She gave him a karate chop right to the chest.

"It's mine," she huffed. "I earned it fair and square. As a detective."

"Cheater! Give me back my uniform!" The guy yanked the green-and-white cap off Mimi's head. He tore at the apron.

"I'll sue you!" she screamed. "My parents are lawyers!"

I'd been so busy watching the cat-and-dog fight that I hadn't noticed Bubba Joe Spikes running toward us.

"Here." He shoved an enormous plastic bag of popcorn against my stomach. It must have been four feet long. "Hold this," he said, dancing back and forth from one foot to the other. "I gotta go bad." Before I could react, he disappeared around the corner of the car wash in the direction of the rest rooms.

I stared numbly at the popcorn, wondering why I'd been dumb enough to let Bubba Joe get away before I'd made him tell me exactly what the Spikeses were up to. Without warning, someone a lot bigger than Bubba Joe grabbed me. I lost my balance and nearly fell to the ground as he spun me around.

"Where did that kid go?" The guy was wearing a red vest that I recognized right away as the uniform from Smith's Food King.

I figured he meant Bubba Joe. "The boys' bathroom."

Without so much as a thank you, the man darted after him.

Mimi and the car washer continued their argument.

"There," she said, handing over the sunglasses. "I hope you're satisfied."

"Well, I'm not," he yelled. "You owe me at least half. That guy wouldn't of give you nothing if I hadn't of let you work for me. You gotta give me at least two-fifty."

"I do not. I was the one who did the work."

Yelling seemed to be popular right at that minute. The man from the grocery store came back and started yelling at me. "You're lying. The two of you are in cahoots. He isn't in the men's room."

"Well, that's where he said he was going."

"Is he your brother?"

"No."

"Do you know him?"

"Yes."

"Hah! I thought so. Well, you can just come with me to the manager's office."

"What for?"

"Stolen property." He nodded toward the bag of popcorn.

"Bubba Joe stole this?"

"I saw him do it with my own eyes." The man's fingers were wound so tightly around my arm that I knew it would be the color of blueberries in the morning. "And if you're lying for him, you're guilty, too." He gave me a shove. "Come on."

"I didn't lie. Honest." I turned to Mimi and the car washer for support. "Bubba Joe said he was going to the bathroom, didn't he?"

"How should I know?" asked the guy.

Mimi shrugged.

"They were busy when Bubba Joe came up to

me," I explained to the man. "I guess they didn't hear."

"I guess not," he replied sarcastically. "Come on."

I couldn't leave right then. DeVeda and Calvin could come out of the pizza store at any minute. And I was still hoping to nab Bubba Joe and talk to him alone.

I didn't move.

"Now," the man insisted.

"I can't come now. I've got to talk to Bubba Joe, too. Even worse than you do."

"Don't play games with me, young lady."

I looked at the five-dollar bill, feeling torn. Well, I'd lived for nearly thirteen years with hair that wasn't bouncy or full and didn't shine like a shampoo model's. I figured I could live with it a little while longer. "How about if I pay for the pop-corn?"

"Wel-l-l . . ."

I looked again at the money. Easy come, easy go, I thought. "Is this enough?"

He made a face. "Yeah. But you'll still have to come to the store with me. I don't have any change here."

"Keep it."

The man accepted the money. "All right." He started toward Smith's and then called back over his shoulder, "But don't think you and your little friend can ever pull a stunt like this again. Next time I'm calling the cops." He jogged off toward the grocery store.

Cripes.

As soon as the checker had left, the car washer took up his own argument with Mimi. Exactly where he'd left off. "You could at least give me half of that fiver."

"If I gave you half, how could I frame this five-dollar bill and save it as, like, a keepsake for the rest of my life?"

I felt a punch in my back. Bubba Joe was back. "Gimme that popcorn!" He tugged at the bag, but I held on tight.

"Where have you been?" I demanded.

"I told you already. In the bathroom."

"You were not. The man from Smith's looked."

"I didn't say I was going in the *boys'* bathroom. I'm no dummy. I knew where he'd look. Now give me my popcorn."

"It's mine," I said. "I paid for it."

"It is not. It's mine. I found it." He ducked his head. He looked up at me through his eyelashes. And then he kicked. My leg felt as if I'd been attacked by an NHL goalie swinging a steel hockey stick.

"Ow!" I cried, reaching down to rub my shin. "Ow! Ow! Ow!"

Bubba Joe seized the moment. Also the popcorn. In the scuffle the plastic bag ripped, spraying white flowerets in every direction. I fell to the ground.

All of a sudden DeVeda and Calvin came out of the pizza store and climbed into the T-bird. *Vrmmm. Vrmmm. Screech.* The car lurched forward.

Without Bubba Joe.

"Wait for me!" He waved the bag into the air. "Wait for me!" he cried again as the car burped and sputtered through the parking lot and turned right into the street. Bubba Joe ran toward the car, his thongs going *slap, slap, slap* on the asphalt.

I struggled to my feet, but the instant I put any weight on my leg it felt as if it were on fire. Darn you, Bubba Joe Spikes! I thought. Darn you!

I turned around. "Mimi!" I barked. "Go catch him!"

Bubba Joe was still waving his plastic bag in the air. *Slap, slap, slap, slap!* He ran furiously after the T-bird, leaving a trail of popcorn behind.

13

Mimi brushed past me and raced through the parking lot after Bubba Joe, her long legs as graceful as a gazelle's.

"Hurry!" I yelled. "Hurry!"

Watching her, I was sure Bubba Joe didn't have a chance. With those long legs, Mimi would catch up to him in no time and hold him until I limped up, too. In my mind I could see Mimi and me playing good cop–bad cop and giving Bubba Joe the third degree until he spilled everything: what the Spikeses had already done to Ashlee Brinkerhoff and what the rest of DeVeda's plans were to get me elected queen of the fall dance with Earl the Hurl.

Far ahead, Bubba Joe had now turned onto the sidewalk and was chugging along Sixth East. He kicked off his thongs so he could run faster, but he wouldn't let go of the plastic bag, even though you could tell he was having trouble running with the awkward thing. And sooner or later he'd be sorry he'd stolen it because he wasn't going to be able to eat much of its contents. Little dribbles of popcorn trailed behind him, like pebbles set by a troop of Boy Scouts marking a trail.

Smiling to myself, I watched Mimi gaining on him.

But no sooner had I limped onto the sidewalk than our luck changed. A yellow car careened along the street to my left. A yellow *Thunderbird* with three redheaded kids inside. DeVeda must have realized she was missing one of her passengers and driven around the block to come back for him.

The car whinnied and lurched until it came to an abrupt stop just ahead of Bubba Joe. As Bubba Joe caught up to it, the back door swung open. Earl reached out, snatching the popcorn with one hand and Bubba Joe's wrist with the other, and pulled him aboard.

Mimi leaned forward for a last-minute sprint, but she wasn't fast enough. The T-bird screeched off and barreled through a red light, its rear door swinging back and forth. As Earl reached over to slam it shut, I saw Bubba Joe looking out the rear window. He stuck out his tongue at Mimi and wiggled his fingers from both ears.

For a few yards Mimi chased after the disappearing car, but anyone could see she'd never catch up. At last she collapsed on the grass along the side of the road.

Cripes. How could we ever catch the Spikes bandits without a car of our own to follow them in?

Vroom—Vroom—Vroom!

There it was. Rescue from heaven. A motorcycle cop pulled up on my left, his progress slowed by cars in front of him, which were waiting for the red light. He put down a foot to steady his bike as it idled and then looked leisurely from side to side as if he were taking a sightseeing tour up Big Cottonwood Canyon and it wasn't his business to worry about the twelve-year-old beetlebrain up ahead who had just driven a stolen car through a red light in the middle of rush-hour traffic.

I waved my arms and hollered, "Follow that yellow car. It's stolen. And the crazy driver just went through a red light."

At least that's what I meant to say. But I guess I was just too rattled to talk straight. What came out sounded more like "Follow that yellow driver. It's red. And the crazy popcorn just went through a stolen light."

He grinned, showing a row of ninety million white teeth. Then, as if I were a four-year-old selling mudpies, he dismissed me with a wave of his hand and zoomed off on his motorcycle.

It was hard to believe that my perfect opportunity had just sailed away like that. Now there wasn't much else to do but catch up with Mimi and try to cheer her up. Or hope she'd cheer me up.

On the way I passed Bubba Joe's black thongs and for no reason bent over to pick them up. No wonder he'd had trouble running in them. They were so big they would have fit an ape. And just as smelly, too. I dropped them pronto once I accidentally got a whiff.

By then Mimi had rested all she needed to. She jumped to her feet and ran to meet me. "Did you see her? Did you see her?"

I nodded. "She drove right through a red light. She's absolutely the worst driver in—"

"Not DeVeda. Ashlee. Did you see Ashlee?"

"Ashlee? Where?"

"On the floor in back. Her hands were tied together."

Shivers ran down my back. "Are you sure?"

"I'm sure I saw a pair of hands tied together. Someone was obviously, like, lying on the floor. Who else's could they have been?"

I didn't know. I didn't know anything except that we needed help. From someone with a car. "Where could Mom be?" I complained.

"When did you call her?"

"Nearly an hour ago. She should have been here by now. Let's go back to the mall and look for her."

It didn't take long. The first thing I saw as we approached the strip mall was Mama's white Celebrity parked in front of the pizza takeout. She was standing beside it, looking anxiously at her watch.

"Where have you been?" she asked.

"Where have *you* been?" I retorted.

"You told me to meet you at the strip mall at Sixth South and Fourth East, but there wasn't one there. So I drove around and around looking for you until I finally figured out you meant Sixth East and Fourth South."

I opened my mouth to argue, then quickly shut it again. I didn't think I could have made such a dumb mistake, but maybe I had, considering what I'd told that motorcycle cop.

Mama looked around. "I thought you said the Spikes children would be here."

"You missed them. They just left."

"Don't tell me they took off in Mrs. Overfield's car!"

"Uh-huh. They went down Sixth East," I said, pointing. "DeVeda was driving."

"I hope she wasn't speeding again the way she did last summer. I'll never forgive myself if she crashes."

"She probably will," I said. "She drove right through a red light."

"Good heavens. What about that girl you said they'd taken with them? That friend of yours—Ashlee Something-or-other—was she still with them?"

"Ashlee Brinkerhoff," Mimi said breathlessly. "She was all tied up as if they, like, planned to torture her. It was un-*real*!"

Mama gasped. "Torture! I really don't think the Spikes children would torture anyone. Would they?"

"I saw her myself," Mimi said, "on the floor of the car. She was, like, all tied up."

"You think you saw some hands tied up," I reminded her. "You don't know they were Ashlee's. They could have been a big doll's, maybe, or a mannequin's."

"Oh, please!" Mimi said sarcastically. "Just why would they tie up a doll's hands?"

"No, I'm almost sure they wouldn't torture anyone," Mama assured herself. "Calvin wouldn't,

120

anyway. He was so sweet with Mrs. Overfield's cats last summer." Mama turned to me. "You don't really think any of them would hurt Ashlee, do you?"

I bit my lip. Who knew what the Spikes kids would do?

Mimi's imagination was racing ninety miles an hour. "I bet they're at least planning to, like, starve her. I bet they're planning to keep her hands and legs tied up and not give her anything to eat but bread and water until she, like, agrees to do everything they tell her. Or maybe, like, starves to death."

"Oh, no, I don't—" Mama began.

"If only we knew where to look for them," I said.

"I'm hungry," Mimi said.

Mama closed her eyes and sniffed the air. "Mmm," she agreed.

You had to admit the yeasty, spicy smells coming from the pizza takeout would have made anyone hungry right then, even if Mimi hadn't been getting us all worked up about food. My stomach growled, reminding me that I hadn't eaten anything all day but a bowl of breakfast cereal.

Mimi pulled the five-dollar bill out of her pocket, biting the insides of her cheeks as she studied it. Anyone else who had just received an unexpected five dollars and was standing in front of a great-smelling pizza takeout with two other hungry people might have offered to treat the crowd. Or at least go Dutch. Not Mimi. For a kid with the biggest allowance this side of Beverly Hills, Mimi Saltzgiver is tighter than a nuclear submarine. She stuffed the money back in her pocket and looked shyly at the back of her hand. Her fingernails, speckled with raspberry-red polish, were chewed to the quick.

Mama cleared her throat. "I don't suppose one slice of pizza each would spoil our dinners." She nodded toward the takeout. "Let's go in there and see if they'll sell it that way. I'll just grab my research notebook from the car and jot down all the important facts you can tell me about the Spikeses while we eat."

No matter what she said about not believing that the Spikes kids would torture anyone, I could tell from the look on her face that Mama was worried. Both Ashlee Brinkerhoff and Mrs. Overfield's car were in trouble. So were we.

14

Knitting her brows together, Mama pulled one of those big pads of lined yellow paper from the car, tucked it under her arm, and locked up the Celebrity. Then she headed toward the door of the pizza takeout, her nose pointing the way like the snout of a bloodhound. Mimi and I followed.

Inside, a ceiling fan whirled above our heads without doing much to lower the temperature. A fly buzzed noisily against the window. Mimi and I sat down at one of the little white Formica tables while Mama walked over to the counter to place our order.

She returned with three slices of ham-and-pineapple pizza and then flipped open the yellow pad to a blank page. "So-o-o," Mama said, "if the two of you had just kidnapped someone in a stolen 1965 automobile, where would you go?"

Mimi drew her chair closer, ducked her head, and spoke softly. "That depends."

"On what?" I asked.

"On how much money I had, like, to charter an airplane. Or if I knew someone who could forge a really fabulous passport. Or—"

Sometimes I wondered if Mimi didn't read too many mystery novels. "Get real," I told her. "It's a bunch of kids we're dealing with here—four juvenile airheads."

"Oh, I don't know about that," Mimi argued. "DeVeda's not so dumb. You said she, like, built a stink bomb in Ashlee's locker. I bet you couldn't do that."

I shrugged.

"I wouldn't be surprised if she grows up to, like, mastermind an international spy ring," Mimi continued. "I've been reading this really fabulous book about an international lady spy and DeVeda reminds me of her so much it's un-*real*."

Mama's pen sketched a fury of spirals and twists and squiggles across the page as she took everything down in her personal shorthand.

Mimi looked over her shoulder and then spoke so softly that I could hear the shuddery noises Mama's felt-tip pen was making. "And Bubba Joe is, like, what psychologists call a 'fiendishly clever sociopath.' "

I hadn't known that Mimi enjoyed self-help psychology books. Maybe she read too many of those, too. "He's the most fiendishly clever sociopath I ever met," she went on. "Have you ever noticed that he does, like, the exact opposite of what a normal person would do?"

Mama's pen kept zipping across her notepad while she contributed an opinion of her own. "Well, I'm not sure I'd put it that strongly about Bubba Joe. But Calvin's very intelligent. You have to be intelligent to train a *cat.*"

I noticed that no one seemed to admire Earl's brains. He was the oldest of the Spikes kids and should have been the smartest, but I decided not to point that out. I didn't want to remind them that the only person who wanted to run for king of the fall dance with me was a guy who didn't have enough smarts to spell his own name and scratch his elbow at the same time.

"So-o-o," Mama said again, rephrasing her question, "if the two of you belonged to the Spikes family, where would you take a stolen 1965 Thunderbird and a classmate you had just kidnapped?"

"Home," Mimi said.

"Home?" I snorted. "That's the first place people would look."

"But sociopaths are clever, remember," Mimi argued. "They'd go home to trick you because you'd never expect them to be so, like, obvious. Anyway, I bet the Spikeses don't live in a *normal* house. I bet it's full of secret passages and little trapdoors and cold dungeon rooms in the basement that are, like, full of black widow spiders. And they'll put Ashlee in one of them and they'll chain her and give her nothing to eat but bread and water and maggoty stew on rusty old pie tins."

Mama's eyes widened and with one finger she pushed her pizza crust farther away. I was glad I'd finished eating, even though I didn't really figure those Spikes kids would do any of the things Mimi had said or that their house was different from anyone else's.

"If only we knew where they lived," Mimi complained, "we could drive there and pretend to be inspectors from the government's Office of Safety and Health Administration and search their whole house."

"But we don't," I said. "I looked in the phone book last summer and there wasn't any Spikes family listed." Then I suddenly remembered something. "Hey! We can telephone! I have their phone number on the note Earl gave me today!"

"That's right," Mimi said excitedly. "You could

disguise your voice and pretend you're, like, a judge from the Red's contest and ask where they live."

I raised my hand for a high-five with her. Then I removed my backpack, unfastened the Velcro, and found Earl's love letter and a quarter. Remembering that I had seen a pay telephone outside the restaurant, I rushed out the door to dial the number.

At last I heard a recorded message: "At the request of the customer the number you dialed has been changed. You may want to check the number and try again."

My quarter clanked back into the return slot. I dialed again. Same message.

Cripes. Earl had given me the number only a couple of hours earlier. I wondered how long those people kept a telephone number, for heaven's sakes, and if the Red's girl had reached Mrs. Spikes.

When I reported the bad news, Mimi had still another suggestion. "We'll just have to go door to door until we find where they live. That's what Kinsey Millhone would do." She turned to Mama. "Don't you just love the Kinsey Millhone mysteries?"

Mama's a big fan of those books, too, and I half expected her to launch into one of her discussions about plot and character and motivation and figures of speech, which can go on and on for about twenty years, but she didn't. "Oh, we could never do that," she said. "There are thousands of doors in Salt Lake alone, not counting the ones in Sandy or West Valley City or—"

"Maybe we're letting our imaginations run away from us," I said. "Maybe the Spikeses just borrowed Mrs. Overfield's car for a little while and have already taken it back to the Greyhound Bus depot. Maybe they took Ashlee home first."

"What? They'd never do anything like that," said Mimi, sounding disappointed. "They're Spikeses, remember?"

"Yeah, maybe," I agreed. "But it would be pretty dumb of us to spend all night looking for Ashlee if she's already home. I'm going to try to call her."

I thumbed through the phone book until I found a Brinkerhoff family on Eighteenth Avenue, where I was pretty sure Ashlee lived. I dialed the number and waited.

A woman finally answered. "Hello." It sounded like Ashlee's mother. Her voice had exactly the same sweet-and-sour ring that Ashlee used when she wanted you to know that your new haircut didn't suit your face or your earrings had gone out of style.

"Hello. Is Ashlee there?"

"No, I'm afraid she isn't. Would you care to leave a message?"

"Uh . . ." I wasn't sure if I should give my right name or not. I decided to use a first name only. "This is Kim. Do you know how I can reach her?"

"Not right now, Kim. She isn't available by phone. Now if you'd please excuse me . . ." Mrs. Brinkerhoff sounded frantic, the way Mama does when she has a story deadline in forty-eight hours and her computer printer won't work.

"Is there some way I can reach her?"

"Not until Monday."

My heart sank.

"She's staying up the canyon with a girlfriend," Mrs. Brinkerhoff continued. "Now I really have to go. We're having dinner guests in ten minutes, and I haven't—"

"Please, Mrs. Brinkerhoff! Don't hang up! I think Ashlee's been kidnapped!"

"What?"

"I saw it with my own eyes. Some kids forced her into a car in the school parking lot. Right after school."

"Did you say *kids*?"

"Yes. They—"

"I'm sure they weren't forcing her, Kim. Ashlee

packed her duffel bag this morning and put it in the trunk of her friend's car when they drove to Bryant this morning. Ashlee's planning to spend the weekend in a Brighton cabin with a girl from West High who's helping her work up a new routine for the cheerleading finals on Monday."

"No, it wasn't the girl from West who took her. It was some younger kids. The Spikeses. They have red hair and their names are Earl and DeVeda and—"

"I'm sure you're mistaken, Kim. Ashlee called me right after school to remind me that she was going up the canyon with her friend Jennifer."

"Well, can you give me Jennifer's phone number, please? I really need to find out if Ashlee's all right."

"I'm sure she is. Anyway, both the city and cabin telephones are unlisted. I really can't give the numbers out."

I thought fast. "Would you please telephone Ashlee and then call me back to let me know—"

"Dorothy," a male voice yelled from the background. "I need you to come taste this barbecue sauce."

"I'm sorry, Kim. You'll have to excuse me." And the phone went dead.

I stared at the receiver, wondering why I should worry about the most stuck-up girl in the entire universe if her very own mother didn't care about her.

"Well?" Mimi asked. "What did she say?"

"She didn't believe me," I reported numbly.

Mimi wrung her hands. "What can we do now?"

We both looked at Mama.

Mama, who thinks best when she's chewing, just shrugged and pulled a fresh pack of Big Red out of her purse to pass around. When Mimi and I refused, Mama unwrapped every single stick and popped them into her own mouth. No kidding. Five sticks all at once. *Chomp, chomp, chomp.*

Mimi's eyeballs grew to the size of avocado pits, but for once she couldn't think of anything to say. Mama kept on chewing.

I finally realized that I was still holding the receiver and slammed it onto the hook. "Well, I quit."

"You can't quit!" Mimi wailed. "This is, like, the most important case I've ever been involved in."

Mama put her arm around me. "Of course you can't quit. Not when an innocent girl has been kidnapped. Not when Mrs. Overfield's wonderful old car has been stolen. Why, it could be speeding toward destruction right this minute."

"I suppose," I said with a sigh, but not because I agreed with Mama's description of Ashlee. "Well, there's only one thing left for us to do. We've got to report the Spikes kids to the police."

"Un-*real!*" Mimi said.

Mama squinched her face up into a mass of wrinkles more zig-zaggedy than a road map of Los Angeles County. I figured she was wondering the same thing I was. Would the police pay any more attention to us now than they had last summer? Every time we'd tried to report any of the sixty million crimes the Spikes kids had committed in July, the police had just rolled their eyes at the ceiling or yawned behind their hands or—worst of all—laughed at us, louder than a pack of hyenas, as soon as we left the room.

"All right," Mama said through her mouthful of Big Red. "We'll take Mimi home so her parents won't worry and then go to the police station."

"Ooh!" Mimi wailed. "I've never been inside a police station. And I need to learn all about them if I'm going to be a lady P.I. when I grow up. Take me with you."

I was tempted to point out that the Salt Lake City desk sergeants aren't very friendly to repeat complainers, like my mother and me, and Mimi would probably have more fun doing her police research from some Kinsey Millhone mystery books. But I decided to let her find that out for herself.

Mama kept chewing.

"My parents won't worry," Mimi argued. "They have a Bar Association dinner tonight, and all I was planning to do was, like, nuke something in the microwave and watch reruns on TV."

"Well . . ." With a thumb and a forefinger, Mama pulled the gooey pink blob from her mouth, wrapped it in a scrap of paper from her purse, and dumped it into a garbage can. "Okay. But I want you to check in with them, anyway."

Mimi agreed. After she got off the phone, Mama called Dad at his office, letting him know that we'd be late and telling him how to reheat the casserole from dinner last night. One good thing about having a workaholic art-history professor for a father is that he always has reading and writing to catch up on and doesn't throw a fit if you leave him alone once in a while.

"Look! Someone's having a yard sale," Mimi reported as we headed toward the Celebrity. "I just love to look at the old jewelry they have at yard sales."

"Yard sale?" I repeated. I'd been planning what we could say to the desk sergeant so that the police would believe us this time. I couldn't figure out what she was talking about.

"There's a flier under your windshield wiper," Mimi said. "People holding yard sales always go to, like, strip-mall parking lots so that they can put fliers under the windshield wipers of all the cars."

I reached for the yellow paper under the wiper. The note was printed in uneven letters with a black felt-tip pen, and Mimi read it aloud over my shoulder:

Kim—

Dont waste your time following us no more. Your job is to practise for Monday so you can be a chear-leader. Us kids will take care of Ashly so you and Earl can be lovers at the fall dance and forever.

D, C & BJ

P.S. It is a far, far better thing we do than we have ever done. And it is a far, far worster place we take her than she has ever seen.

"If DeVeda wrote this, she may be dumber than I thought," Mimi said. "She won't be able to master-mind an international spy ring until she learns how to spell."

"Goodness!" exclaimed Mama. "Are you going to the fall dance with Earl Spikes?"

I didn't know whether to scream or cry or throw up. "No! Of course not!" I squared my shoulders and gave Mimi a shove. We had to get into the car and head to the police station.

Fast.

15

▰ ▰ ▰ ▰ ▰ ▰ ▰ ▰ ▰ ▰ ▰ ▰ ▰ ▰

I reached into the backseat for Mama's white jacket before climbing out of the Celebrity. "Here," I said. "Put this on."

She was already on the sidewalk after parking the car on Fifth South, across the street from the police station. "Oh, I don't need a jacket. It's not cold outside."

"No, but maybe the jacket will hide your T-shirt."

Mama looked down. "Oh, my goodness. I forgot I was wearing this."

How could anyone forget a T-shirt like *that*? I wouldn't have worn it on Halloween. It was a hideous shade of purple with an orange fox on the front. And printed underneath was a message you wouldn't believe: I'M A SUPER FOX—FROM ELDRED B. FOX ELEMENTARY SCHOOL.

To judge from the T-shirts in her closet, you'd think that Mama had attended every elementary school in the country. But the shirts are just presents that the principals have given her when she's visited their schools to talk about books. She has enough foxes and bears and cougars to populate Yellowstone National Park.

Most of them aren't too bad, but I didn't think I'M A SUPER FOX would make a very good impression on the police.

"Please, Mom. Put the jacket on. And button it all the way," I said. "You've got to look serious if you want the desk sergeant to believe you this time."

"Oh, Kim!" Mama wailed, but she started buttoning.

The jacket covered some of the writing but not all of it. I studied her for a minute. I'm used to the way she dresses, so I sometimes forget about how Mama must appear to other people. Fifty-five years old. Hair of no particular color. Five feet tall and one-hundred-forty pounds. It's amazing that anyone who eats as little as she does could be so heavy. She may be the only person in the entire world who's gained forty extra pounds from chewing gum. But I wouldn't trade her for anything. Whenever I need her she's there for me.

"That's better," I said. "More professional. Now give me your notepad."

Mama held it out. "What do you need it for?"

"I don't, but neither do you." I didn't want to hurt her feelings, but she needed to know the truth. "Nobody takes you seriously when you're jotting down research notes all the time. The policemen laughed every time we came to the station last summer."

"But what will I do if I ever decide to write a book about a police station and need some Life-Experience notes?"

"You took Life-Experience notes at the police station three times last summer. Use those." I put the notepad on the front seat, set the lock, and slammed the door. "I won't let them laugh at you again."

"They weren't laughing about my notes. They were laughing because Mrs. Overfield's house and car had been taken over by four . . . four . . ." —Mama hesitated, temporarily at a loss for words— "children!—and we didn't know how to evict them."

"Well, how do you suppose the police are going to react when we tell them those same four *children* have kidnapped someone? We've got to do everything differently this time. We've got to act serious and professional."

Mama sighed but didn't say anything else. She just trotted silently at my side—across the street, across the plaza, and along the pathway marked by arrows to the police station complaint desk—as Mimi set the pace with her long strides.

Once we reached the complaint desk there was bad news and good news.

The bad news was that the sergeant sitting there was the same man Mama and I had already met on two of our three earlier visits to the station. Even though he didn't look up right away, I recognized him by the way his big head rested on his shoulders, like the head of one of those wild buffaloes you see in old black-and-white movies.

The good news was that he didn't seem to recognize Mama and me.

Maybe he was confused because Mimi was along this time and there were three complainers instead of only two. Maybe he was too busy punching information into his computer to recognize anyone.

He looked up at us just long enough to see that we didn't have any obvious injuries, like multiple bullet holes or gushing butcher-knife wounds, before he turned back to his computer screen. "Yes?" he mumbled in a deep voice. More like a moose than a buffalo.

"I'm Janice Burgener Sanders, a freelance writer and lecturer," Mama began, and you couldn't help feeling proud of how professional she sounded. "My husband is an art-history professor at the University of Utah. I'm here to report a kidnapping."

"Kidnapping?" The sergeant must have been a little bit interested in kidnappings, because he lifted his big head to look Mama straight in the eye. "Are you sure?"

"Of course I'm sure. My daughter and her friend here saw the abduction with their own eyes. The victim is named Ashlee Brinkerhoff and she's a student at Bryant Junior High School."

"Junior high?" he repeated, shaking his head. "Disgusting. I have a daughter of my own in junior high. Hardly dare let her out of my sight with all the perverts running loose." He punched a couple of keys on his computer and his screen went black. In a second it turned pale blue again. "All right. How do you spell the victim's name?"

Mimi was only too happy to help. "A-S-H-L-E-E B-R-I-N-K-E-R-H-O-F-F."

"She's thirteen years old. Just like me." Mimi nodded in my direction. "Kim won't be thirteen for nearly two weeks."

I scowled.

"Perverts," the sergeant mumbled as he typed. "The whole city is full of perverts." He looked up. "I need her parents' names and their address."

Now it was my turn to answer since I'd looked up that information less than an hour earlier.

The policeman typed everything I told him and then wiped his mouth with a handkerchief. There was a line of complainers forming behind us, but the sergeant didn't seem to care. Our complaint was more important.

"I'll need complete statements from both of the witnesses, but first let me have your names and addresses." He looked at Mimi. "You first."

"I'm Mimette Saltzgiver, but everyone calls me Mimi. Even teachers. I live at 1620 Arlington Drive. You probably know my parents, Gerald and Carol Saltzgiver. They're both lawyers. Saltzgiver and Saltzgiver."

"I can't say that I do," he said. But he typed in the information, anyway. "And your name?" he asked me.

"Kimberly Sanders, 1226 Federal Way."

"Kimberly Sanders. That sounds familiar."

"Yes, Sanders and Kimberly are both very common names," Mama said quickly. "And I'm sure you meet lots of people." Good old Mama.

The sergeant shrugged and turned back toward me. "Tell me exactly what you saw."

"Well, Mimi and I were looking out the window of the media center at Bryant and we saw some kids in the parking lot forcing Ashlee into a car."

"Kids?"

"Yes."

"The perverts are *kids*?" He shouted so loudly that everyone behind us could hear what he said.

"Yes." I lowered my voice, hoping he'd get the hint.

"About how old are they?"

"Well, I think Bubba Joe is, like, five," Mimi offered. "And Calvin is seven or eight. And—"

"Five and seven!" he shouted again. "Two kids five and seven kidnapped a thirteen-year-old?"

The people in line behind us tittered.

"Not by themselves," I added quickly. "They were with their big brother and sister. DeVeda and Earl. Earl is really strong."

"He's probably older than we are," Mimi butted in again, "but he's in the same grade we are because he had to repeat seventh—"

The sergeant read aloud from his computer screen. "'Kimberly Sanders.'" Then he stared at me. "Didn't you come in here last summer?"

"Uh, yes."

"Several times?"

"Yes."

"I remember you and your mother." He shot a look in Mama's direction, trying not to smile. "You said a gang of midgets—named Spikes, wasn't it?—had broken into your neighbor's house and wouldn't let you in to—to feed the cats?"

Mama cleared her throat nervously. "They weren't midgets. We . . . um . . . found out later that they were children. Three brothers and a sister."

"And weren't there some plants you were worried about feeding, too?" the sergeant asked, loud enough so that every single person in the entire building could hear his mooselike voice. "Some meat-eating plants?"

Now he was really smiling. Very impolitely. I wondered what a person could do to report impolite desk sergeants who talked too loudly and never took your complaints seriously and laughed at you for wanting to take good care of your neighbor's cats and exotic houseplants.

"Venus's-flytraps," I said. "They eat insects."

"Well, have you seen those . . . those Spikes children lately?"

"Yes, we have," Mimi volunteered. "They're the ones who, like, kidnapped Ashlee."

"Well, well. I don't suppose they drove off with her in an old yellow Thunderbird they stole from your next-door neighbor?"

"How did you know?" Mimi asked.

I heard laughter from behind us. From the next room, too.

The sergeant covered a smile with his hand. "Just . . . just psychic, I guess."

I wanted to die. I wanted to disappear through the floor and sink two miles underground. I wanted to turn into one of those pointy-eared trolls who live in the center of the earth and never come out except to scare horrible people who deserve it.

My voice rose. "We have proof she was kidnapped. I have the note the kidnappers left right here." I reached into my pocket and handed him the yellow paper. There! That would show him!

The sergeant unfolded the note and read silently, his rude smile widening into the most obnoxious grin I've ever seen in my life. "This Earl—the one you said is so strong—did the two of you have a lovers' quarrel?"

"O-o-oh!" My cheeks felt hot enough to barbecue a T-bone. I'd forgotten that part of the note. I couldn't think of anything to say. I couldn't think of anything to do but turn and run down the hall. I heard Mama's and Mimi's footsteps behind me as they followed.

I guess I wasn't exactly looking where I was going, because I nearly bumped into a policeman who was entering through the door. He must have been a motorcycle cop, because he was carrying a helmet in one hand.

"I'm sorry," I said, trying to brush past him, but he grabbed my arm.

He was grinning at me, too. What was the matter with all the policemen in this city?

"Say, don't I know you?"

Not again! I felt tears of frustration forming in my eyes. "Uh, I don't think so."

"Yes, I do. You're the girl I saw on the street a little while ago. I recognize that shirt from the place where all you brainy people go to school."

I looked down. I was wearing the crimson shirt my sister, Andrea, had sent me from Cambridge, Massachusetts, where she and her husband are in graduate school. It said HARVARD.

The policeman grinned even more broadly. "I don't meet many brainy people in my line of work, so I always remember them. You told me to follow the yellow driver because the crazy popcorn had just gone through a stolen light."

I pulled my arm free. "Excuse me. I've got to go."

With Mama and Mimi close behind, I raced out of the door and onto the plaza. From behind us I heard a duet of guffaws, a bass and a tenor. Plus a chorus of other voices, laughing.

But if I'd thought that life was so bad nothing else could possibly go wrong, I was mistaken. When we reached the Celebrity, there was another yellow paper under the windshield wiper. Reading it was like having your worst possible nightmare come to life.

Kim—

Youll be sorry you went to the police. Anything that happens now is all your folt.

We warned you.

16

The telephone rang. More than once.

I finally groped to answer it. "Hello."

I must have been in a pretty deep sleep, because for a second I couldn't remember what day it was (Sunday) or why I'd gone to bed so early (because I was exhausted after practicing my cheerleading drills with Mimi for two entire days) or why Dad or Mama hadn't answered the phone first (because they'd gone out for the evening with friends).

"Kimberly?" said a gruff voice. The caller was trying to sound like a man, a menacing man. But I knew it was a girl. I even knew *which* girl.

I leaned up on one elbow. "DeVeda! Where are you?"

"None of your business."

"What have you done with Ashlee?"

"You *are* nosy, aren't you?"

I sat up in bed. "I just want to know if she's all right. Is she?"

"Didn't you get the notes me and the others put on your car?"

"Two. I got two."

"Well, then—"

"Well, *what?*"

"If you don't want to be held responsible for that Ashlee's permanent disappearance—"

I knew it! The Spikeses had figured out some way to implicate me in the kidnapping!

"—if you ever want to see her again," DeVeda continued, "you'll do your part. You'll go to those tryouts tomorrow and get yourself on the cheer-leading squad so you and Earl—"

"Just tell me if Ashlee is all right."

"Who cares if Ashlee is all right? That prissy Barbie doll is stubborner than a one-eyed mule. Do you have any clue of what me and Calvin and Bubba Joe has had to put up with for two and a half days just so's you and Earl can be lovers?"

I didn't know which point to deal with first: what I figured Ashlee's captors had been forced to put up with or what chance there was on the entire planet Earth that Earl Spikes and I would ever become lovers.

"That Ashlee is the whiniest hostage anyone ever took," DeVeda went on. "She whines 'cause she don't have no bubblebath nor hairspray. She whines 'cause she don't have no television so's she can watch her favorite rock stars on MTV. She whines 'cause the peanut-butter sandwiches I sneak in to her are made with the wrong brand."

At least Ashlee was being fed. That relieved me. A little.

"Me and Calvin and Bubba Joe are plain down-right sick of her," DeVeda continued. "We'd drive her to Las Vegas and dump her right this minute if we had enough money for gasoline."

I sat on the edge of the bed. "Don't do that, DeVeda! Don't do anything that stupid!"

"Yeah," DeVeda agreed. "That would be dumb, all right. If we dropped her by the side of the road, she'd just hold out her thumb until someone with a cellular phone came by. Then she'd call that daddy of hers and make him send her enough money for a plane ticket to fly back to Bryant tomorrow before the tryouts. Me and Calvin and Bubba Joe has just got to try and put up with her another day until after the tryouts are over."

"No, you don't. Let her go to the tryouts, DeVeda. It's only fair. I wouldn't want to win if I couldn't do it fairly. Besides," I lied, "Earl and I can be friends even if I'm not a cheerleader."

I waited for DeVeda to respond, and when she didn't I went on talking. "I don't really care if I make the squad. There are lots of things I'd rather do, anyway. My friends Mimi and Darci are the ones who wanted me to be on the team. They talked me into it."

For several seconds there was dead silence on the line. I almost wondered if the connection had been broken.

At last DeVeda spoke again—in a voice like a metal file scraping on concrete. "Yes, you *do* want to be a cheerleader. Me and Calvin and Bubba Joe has put up with too much of Ashlee Brinkerhoff's crybaby stubbornness for you to weasel out now. If you don't go to those tryouts tomorrow—and if you don't win—me and my brothers will *find* the money for gasoline. And we'll blindfold Ashlee and we'll tie her up and we won't dump her off until we get all the way to Tijuana, Mexico. And if the police catch us, we'll tell them the whole thing was your idea and that you made us do it."

Slam.

The telephone receiver droned in my hand, but I was too numb to even hang the thing up.

I wished I were smart enough to figure out where

Ashlee was being held. I wished there were some way to trace DeVeda's call. I wished my parents would come home so I wouldn't feel so all alone.

But there was nothing I could do but lie back in bed and try to stop worrying, so that's what I did.

17

It had been only seven days since school started, but I felt as if I'd aged seventy years. Dressed in my freshly laundered white shorts and a brand-new red-and-gray sweatshirt, I stood in the doorway of the gym. Four of the six cheerleading hopefuls were huddled around Miss Hudson, and I decided I should probably join them.

But before I got there, a lady came charging past me on her way to speak to Miss Hudson herself. Her face was the color of spaghetti sauce, and she seemed mad enough to eat hornets. She also looked vaguely familiar, but for the life of me I couldn't remember where I'd seen her before.

"Where are my children?" she demanded, as if Miss Hudson had stolen them, which I personally doubted. Miss Hudson puts up with kids because she has to, but she isn't famous for liking any of them, and I couldn't imagine she'd ever want to live with one.

The teacher looked down over her long nose. "What children?"

"Earl and DeVeda and Calvin and Bubba Joe. I've got to find them! We're late for the judging!" she cried.

Uh-oh. Now I remembered where I'd seen her. From behind the plant in the ZCMI snack bar last summer.

"They don't have red hair, do they?" asked Miss Hudson.

"Yes," said Mrs. Spikes with a big smile, as if Miss Hudson had just complimented those four bratty kids, which of course she hadn't.

"Well, I'm relieved to tell you they're not here," said the teacher.

Somehow Mrs. Spikes must have missed the point of Miss Hudson's remark, because for a minute she turned chatty. "They're supposed to be trying out for the Red's contest," she explained. "Every one of them but Earl. The Red's people said he's too old. But all my children have beautiful red hair, and they'd be perfect for the Red's pictures. Oh, I wish I knew where they were."

Miss Hudson shrugged as if she didn't really care

very much about Earl's age or the Red's contest or beautiful red hair, even. "I'm sure I'd know if they were here."

"Calvin and Bubba Joe promised to meet me outside their school. But when I got there, one of their friends said they'd taken a taxi to come to Bryant to find Earl and DeVeda," Mrs. Spikes continued. "A taxi! All the way from Murray! I just don't understand how their minds work."

Miss Hudson rolled her eyes. You got the feeling that she didn't know how their minds worked, either.

"The workmen are in my kitchen right this minute laying my new parquet floor," Mrs. Spikes said. "I left those men unsupervised in my house to drive all the way from Murray to pick up the children and take them to the judging!"

"Ma'am, if I knew where your children were, I'd be more than happy to turn them over to you. But you can see for yourself that they aren't here." Miss Hudson looked at her watch. "Now if you'll excuse me, I have work to do."

"Of course you do. I'm sorry to interrupt. But if you see my children, please tell them I'm looking for them."

"Count on it."

I felt someone touch my shoulder. "Oh, Kim, I've

been looking all over for you." It was Mrs. Paddock. "I met Mimi Saltzgiver in the hall, and she told me you'd be here. Can we talk?"

"Sure."

"I mean privately."

My throat tightened. Had Mrs. Paddock been concerned about Ashlee's absence today and telephoned Mrs. Brinkerhoff? Had Mrs. Brinkerhoff told her about my phone call on Friday about Ashlee's kidnapping? Would they or Miss Hudson or the principal or anyone in the entire universe believe that I hadn't helped plan the whole ridiculous scheme?

I looked at the clock on the wall of the gym. "Cheerleading tryouts start in ten minutes. If I'm not here when my name is called, I'll be disqualified."

"This won't take long." Mrs. Paddock nodded to her left. "Let's go into the classroom next door."

I followed her into the room, and she motioned for me to sit down beside her.

"I have some very disturbing news to tell you, Kim. About Ashlee Brinkerhoff."

My heart thumped.

"I don't know how to break it gently, so I'll just have to tell you straight. But first I must swear you to secrecy. Will you promise not to tell anyone?"

"Uh, yes. I promise."

Mrs. Paddock cleared her throat. "Ashlee's essay–the one she submitted for the *Bulletin* editorship—was plagiarized. I found the very same article in an old *Reader's Digest.* She'd copied it word for word from an article about environmental protection."

For some reason, that didn't surprise me a whole lot, but I couldn't think of anything to say that wouldn't make me sound snotty.

"Do you still want to be the editor?" Mrs. Paddock asked.

Did I still want to be the editor? Do sharks swim? Are fires hot? Did Bryant Junior High School deserve a better newspaper than the one Ashlee Brinkerhoff could produce in five hundred zillion years?

I grinned. "Of course!"

"Well, then, the job is yours. On one condition."

"What's that?" I asked.

"This story isn't to go beyond this room. I've already talked to the principal, and she agrees with me. Of course we'll speak to Ashlee—speak very strongly about what she did. But we don't want to tarnish her reputation unnecessarily. Something like this might be hard for her to live down if other students knew about it. We want to give her the opportunity to turn her priorities around."

Fat chance, I thought.

Mrs. Paddock bent closer and looked me in the eyes. "I know you've promised me once, but I want you to say it again."

"I promise. I won't tell anyone—except maybe my mother if that's all right—about Ashlee's essay."

Mrs. Paddock nodded. "Yes, you can tell your mother. I'm sure she'll be discreet." She stood up and extended her hand for me to shake. "Well, congratulations, Editor."

"Thank you. Thanks a lot."

I wanted to hug her. I wanted to sing. I wanted to run home and talk to Mama right that minute. But I knew I had to keep my promise to Mimi and Darci about trying out for the cheerleading squad. I walked back to the gym. Lots more people had arrived, but I couldn't see Mrs. Spikes anywhere.

Mimi grabbed my arm. "Where have you been?" she demanded. She nodded toward the center of the gym, where a girl was in the middle of her routine. "This girl is, like, a disaster. I know she'll trip if we try to do any lifts together. I can't have anyone that klutzy for a partner. I'd rather have Ashlee!"

"Well, then, maybe you're in luck," I said, still smiling from my talk with Mrs. Paddock. I nodded toward the four redheads and one brunette walking into the gym right at that moment.

The huge white hair ribbon Ashlee had worn to school on Friday was gone. Her hair was a messy tangle. Her face was streaked with dirt. Her blue shorts looked wrinkled. But she walked courageously, shoulders back. The Spikeses hadn't crushed her. That was the good news.

The bad news was that the Spikes kids seemed to be planning another embarrassing demonstration on my behalf. All of them were carrying pans and spoons or wooden blocks. And tucked under Calvin's arm was a rolled-up banner that undoubtedly said WE ❤ KIM.

I shuddered.

She was pretty far away and I couldn't tell for sure, but I think Miss Hudson may have shuddered, too. Ignoring Ashlee, she stood and walked toward the Spikeses, but I got there first.

"Thanks for listening to me," I told DeVeda. "I'm glad you brought Ashlee back. It's only fair to let her try out."

DeVeda scowled. "You had nothing to do with it."

"It was Earl's idea," said Calvin.

"Only dummies are fair," said Bubba Joe.

Earl refused to look at me. Or anyone else, for that matter. He ducked his head and stuffed his hands in his pockets, standing alone.

Miss Hudson clamped a firm hand on top of Bubba Joe's head. "Your mother's looking for you kids," she said.

"Oh, no, ma'am," said Bubba Joe in his most angelic voice. "She couldn't be."

"We ain't lost," offered Calvin.

"She was here looking for you just a minute ago," Miss Hudson insisted. "She said you're supposed to be at some judging for a Red's contest. So all of you can leave the gym right this minute and go outside to wait for her."

"Oh, no! That wouldn't be a good idea," DeVeda said brightly. "If Mother came looking for us here, this is where she expects us to be. When I went to summer camp two years ago, they told us to stay put if we got lost. 'Hug a tree' they called it."

"Listen, you—" Miss Hudson began. But before she could say whatever it was she wanted DeVeda to listen to, Mrs. Spikes came charging into the gym.

With her were two men wearing jeans, and for a minute I thought she'd driven all the way back to Murray to pick up her parquet floor layers. But then I realized she hadn't had enough time to do that, and besides, the men weren't wearing tool belts or carrying hammers. What they were carrying was a couple of hitchhiking signs that said CHEYENNE and CHICAGO OR BUST.

"There they are!" screamed Mrs. Spikes, pointing at her two younger sons. "Grab them!"

Dropping their signs, the men seized Calvin and Bubba Joe as Mrs. Spikes grabbed DeVeda. "Hurry!" she told her daughter. "We haven't much time."

DeVeda's feet didn't budge. "We want to see the cheerleading tryouts," she complained.

Clang! Bubba Joe dropped a pan as he tried to wriggle free. "We don't want no pictures taken!"

Calvin looked at his mother. "Did Red's promise to give us free cones?" he asked.

Scowling at his captor, Bubba Joe struggled furiously. For a second I thought he was going to kick the poor man. But instead the little maniac broke free and rushed over to where I was standing.

"You dummy!" he cried. And his left toes connected with my right shin.

"OW!" I screamed. "OW! OW! OW!"

I lunged for him, but my leg wouldn't hold my weight, and I fell to the floor. "You little monster!" I shouted, rubbing my leg. Everyone was staring at me, but I went right on yelling. "I can't try out for cheerleading now! My leg is killing me! What did you do that for?"

Bubba Joe grinned. "For Earl."

"For Earl? But I kept my word. I'm here for the tryouts."

"Show her, Calvin." Bubba Joe and his brother each took an end of the banner Bubba Joe was carrying and stretched it out for me to read: WE ♥ ASHLY.

"Earl don't want you here," Calvin reported.

"Earl don't want you to win," Bubba Joe explained.

"When Earl saw Ashlee kick a hole in that shed where we'd hid her, he decided he loves Ashlee more than you," said DeVeda. "He wants her to be on the cheerleading squad."

"So Earl and Ashlee can be lovers," said Calvin.

"Forever," added Bubba Joe.

Across the room I could see Ashlee bending over the judges' table. She didn't look nearly as adorable as she'd been at the first tryouts, and she wasn't carrying any cutesy handouts with full-color computer graphics.

But Earl was watching her every move and drooling like a St. Bernard puppy over its first porterhouse steak.

And in spite of the pain in my leg, in spite of my disgust with Ashlee Brinkerhoff, in spite of my outrage at that horrible Bubba Joe Spikes and the entire gang of loathsome Spikes criminals, I couldn't help smiling.